Love, Unmasked

Vivian Roycroft

δ
Dingbat Publishing

For my Grey, John Grey ("Bond. James Bond."), he of the sweet smile and wicked puns. Love you, Garfield.

And to the Atascocita Culver's crew — Lisa, Don, Haydee, George, Joshua the quiet one, Diana with her beautiful smile, Guillermo who shares my coffee addiction, Ashley who always waves — for creating the perfect atmosphere to soothe a desperate author.

1

Tuesday, December 7, 1813

Fidelity Scott sucked in a shivery breath and froze, knitting needles poised like twin exclamation marks amid her neatly coiled pink yarn. All sensation faded away and around her, the morning room paled to a foggy grey nothingness. The crackling fire warmed her face but lost all color and sound, and the tremor in her hands started in her knitting needles and rippled through to her toes, missing none of her in between.

It happened every time, without fail. Her friend Clarissa Pelham had mentioned *that name*, the one guaranteed to draw Fidelity into dreamy, mindless yearnings no matter the circumstances, and it did so with its usual heady abandon. The raw emotions shivering through her seemed to suck all the bones from her body, leaving her trembling like some loathsome sea creature.

Her younger cousin, Jessica Alcock, sprawled back across the sofa, one arm falling over her face in a pretended swoon, the other grabbing for one of the overstuffed pillows propped among the cushions. The lower half of her face, all that could be seen through her amateur theatrics, seemed to melt into a gooey puddle of drool. "Oooh, yes, Mis-ter Bright-en-burg!" she trilled in a vibrato sing-song.

A chorus of sighs broke through Fidelity's name-induced fog and she shook herself awake. Embarrassing, that was. Honestly, if she couldn't control her reaction when *a certain gentleman's* name was mentioned, then she scored no higher on propriety than her two young cousins, which was very very bad indeed.

At least no one else in the morning room had managed to stay unaffected. On the chair by the hearth, Clarissa stared at the wallpaper, sewing forgotten in her lap and a dreamy expression blanking out her face. The two cousins, younger Jessica and elder Georgette, were too busy indulging each other's overly dramatic silliness to notice anyone else's. Strange, how no one was able to avoid collapsing into a pitiable, quivering mass whenever *that name* was mentioned. Of course, considering the incredible masculinity said name represented... Just the thought moved a few coals from the fireplace to somewhere deep inside her belly.

Georgette squirmed, a single indecorous wriggle of unbearable delight. Several blond curls broke free from her careless knot and dangled around her face, one sporting a forlorn hairpin that swung with her movement. "Oooh, yes, Mister Brightenburg, he of the most delicious legs. What he does to a pair of silken hose and breeches—"

Appalled, Fidelity dropped a stitch. "Georgette!" Not that it wasn't true. But saying it aloud was beyond the pale, even here in the privacy of the morning room. *Although come to think of it, it would be lovely to just hang it all and squirm along with her.* It didn't help that her traitorous thoughts dwelled on the legs in question. Those lovely curving calves, the whip-cord muscular thighs, and above that...

"Indeed!" Jessica flipped upright on the sofa and whirled, grabbing Georgette's shoulders. "Such men should be required by law to wear nothing else."

Fidelity's hands jerked and another loop slid off the needle. *Those girls can't get any worse. It's impossible.*

"Or nothing at all!"

So much for that notion.

The girls collapsed into a single pile of giggling foolishness, blond and brown hair intermixed. Heat climbed Fidelity's cheeks. She was no prude, but those two were becoming more — well, more overtly mature by the day. Thankfully Clarissa was discreet; she'd never gossip about their behavior, at least not with anyone besides Fidelity. *Which is another reason to let go and join them.*

The sudden thought startled her. *Um, no. Actually, it's not.* And now she was arguing with herself.

Fidelity cleared her throat. "Young ladies, neither of you is old enough to be noticing any such thing."

Sudden movement from Clarissa's chair, then a stillness, just as sudden.

Two pairs of blue eyes peered from the heap, artless as kittens and just as innocent. The blond head rose and Georgette propped herself on her elbows atop her sister. "And when shall we be?" she asked, ignoring Jessica's writhing beneath her. "When we're your age, cousin dear?"

Little minx. Fidelity folded her knitting and put it aside. Too much to ask, getting something productive accomplished with those two in the room. "That's unfair. There's only a handful of years between us." And yet, since their governess had left (with a discreet mop of her brow) and their mother refused to come to town, Fidelity now bore responsibility for their education and manners, ensuring their gowns and entertainments were appropriate, and chaperoning them around Mayfair. Just the thought infuriated her.

I am not some pitiful spinster. Not yet, at least.

She hid the shiver. There was nothing wrong with being unmarried at three-and-twenty. It didn't mean she'd never be loved nor have a home of her own. It only meant — well, it only meant she'd not yet married, and nothing more. The right man had come along, but—

Don't be a ninny. It means Sylvestre Brightenburg hasn't proposed yet, and that's because he hasn't noticed you exist.

Clarissa shook out her sewing, a controlled billow of white lawn. "Funny how we never forget our decorum when Mister Greysteil's name is spoken. And yet he's as handsome as Mister Brightenburg, if not more so. I challenge any young lady—" she eyed the girls meaningfully "—to dispute that."

On the sofa, Georgette froze, staring down at her still-flattened sister. Likewise, Jessica stilled her wriggling, staring back. Both creamy foreheads began puckering.

Fidelity flashed Clarissa a tiny smile. Could taming her cousins be so simple?

Then Georgette shrugged and grabbed Jessica's pillow, yanking it away. The shrieking began immediately, the renewed wriggling a second after.

"I must grant you the point, Clarissa," Georgette said through the ruckus. With one hand, she lifted the pillow overhead, out of Jessica's reach; with the other, she propped herself on her sister's midsection, keeping her pinned. "For some reason unknown to womankind, Mister Greysteil of the luscious thick hair and scrumptious green eyes simply does not attract the same level of absorption."

Annoyance flashed through Fidelity's aggravation. John Greysteil had been friends with the two related families, the Scotts and the Alcocks, since Fidelity had turned ten. He deserved more from them than a shrug and a flippant comment. But she had to admit, Georgette had scored, as well: Greysteil reduced none of them to a spineless jellyfish, not even when he smiled.

Perhaps they merely knew him too well. As male animals went, Greysteil was magnificent as a Thoroughbred stallion. But Brightenburg carried an air of mystery and superiority, power and distinction. If Greysteil was a racehorse, Brightenburg was a mustang, unreachable on some thundering Western plain. *With a herd of lusty females galloping along behind him.* Fidelity stifled her snort of laughter. She'd best not share that thought.

Jessica finally shoved Georgette aside and sat up. Her hairpins could claim no more success at keeping her locks in place than her sister's; a brown coil fell to her shoulders and tangled with her fichu, which had been tugged halfway from her gown's neckline. "I challenge any young lady not to notice Mis-ter Brighten-burg."

"Especially his legs," Georgette said.

More giggles. More tugging of the pillow, back and forth between them.

"You rip that pillow, and you replace it." Fidelity sighed and grabbed her knitting. She had two stitches to reinstate.

Jessica released the pillow immediately; she hated

sewing. "Fi, you must admit you've noticed Mis-ter Brightenburg's physical attributes yourself."

Fidelity stiffened, a flush of heat starting in her face. "Whatever do you mean?"

The sound Georgette made could only be described as a whoop. The heat in Fidelity's face intensified.

"Young lady, that racket better becomes some wild creature—" *definitely not a horse* "—rather than a civilized gentlewoman." Granted, they were discussing Georgette. Perhaps she wasn't as cunning as Jessica; she was certainly as spirited. "And I'm sure I don't know what you mean."

Surely no one had noticed her undying devotion to Sylvestre Brightenburg. She'd been discretion itself and couldn't have given herself away.

But Jessica rolled her eyes. "Everyone knows you've set your cap for him, cousin."

The blushing heat, already profound, continued to deepen, and panic licked at her self-control. "That is an execrable expression—"

The girls froze, staring at her.

Horrified, Fidelity broke off. *That vocal sharpness — not acceptable. I'm supposed to be calm, serene, unflappable. Easy to appreciate and love. That temperament's my greatest asset.* She sucked in a deep breath and forced her floundering emotions to heel.

Georgette hugged the pillow to her chest. Her eyes widened as if she watched some dangerous creature stalking them through the morning room. *Or as if one of those galloping mares took a wrong turn toward a cliff.*

Clarissa laid a gentle hand on Fidelity's arm. "When he enters a room, you watch him." Her voice was soft. "Never staring, never anything obvious or gauche. But the rest of us could be discussing the most scintillating subject in England and your responses vary from yes to no, with little variation in between."

She sounds like she's persuading that mare off the precipice. Nice try, Clarissa. "Are you saying everyone — *everyone* — has observed this?" If that were true, calming her would take more than gentle words softly spoken. Fidelity could foresee crashing through a few windows and racing down Piccadilly in a wild panic. Surely her secret was safe—

But Clarissa's small sigh blew that thought out of her head. "Next time he enters a room, Fidelity, dear, try watching the rest of the company instead."

* * * *

four days later,
Saturday, December 11, 1813

At her next opportunity, Fidelity followed Clarissa's advice. She left the entertainment five minutes later, mortified to her bones.

2

four more days later,
Wednesday, December 15, 1813

"What do you mean, you're leaving town? The holiday season's almost here."

The two horses strode side by side along Rotten Row, cool winter sunshine pouring around them like a flood. Bolder riders trotted and cantered past, but the day's brisk beauty and her own roiling, shaken emotions kept Fidelity content with a quiet walk along the rail. No matter how unexciting her current pace, her sweet bay mare, Palfrey, didn't complain. *And for that I'll be grateful. Especially considering Grey's brute.*

John Greysteil again curbed his prancing black stallion, Cassius, forcing the beast into the same slow, staid walk at her mare's side. How long he'd manage that impressive feat was questionable; the stallion seemed ready to explode with restrained energy. Greysteil's hands in their black leather gloves stayed steady and low, his long legs in black breeches and brown-topped boots firm, controlling the stallion with subtlety rather than force. His gaze never left her, mobile brows forming a ruffled bar across his forehead, above his intense green eyes and below the brim of his classical beaver hat. "Well?" he asked.

He'd said something. Oh...

"I mean what I say." She hated the quaver in her voice. But she'd cried herself to sleep every night since that horrible, mortifying evening, even after she'd set her brilliant plan into motion, and her throat felt raw. "Mary is packing, and in a few days two footmen will return to Kent and open the house. Christmas at home will be lovely, and a lovely change." *Father's house, actually.* Not her own, and the sudden, bone-deep yearning for *her* household, *her* husband, *her* children, nearly shook her from the saddle. She swallowed. *Not much chance of that now. I'm as good as ruined, after making such a fool of myself for so long. No wonder I've never received an offer of matrimony.*

Greysteil's fingers flexed around the four reins. The stallion jibbed at the bit, tried to throw his head back, ran into the martingale, and pranced again, frustrated. "But next season—"

"—would be my seventh." Another quaver. She swallowed and tried again. "It will contain the same parties and dinners and dances as the one before, and the one before that, and the one before that. I'm bored, Mister Greysteil."

He shot her a glance and Fidelity swallowed the rest of her prepared excuse. No sense bothering to spew it out; she might pretend to be at peace with her plan, but he knew she lied. He had that look on his face, with his eyebrows starting to arch, his lips set in a thin line, and the first hint of heightened color rising in his stubble-dusted cheeks.

Hopefully he's too much of a gentleman to accuse me to my face. But a coil of some unhappy emotion clutched at her chest and squeezed.

"Something's happened," he said, quietly, but not so quietly that she wasn't supposed to hear it.

Hoofbeats rolled behind them; he curbed the stallion in advance and held him — in place if not still — as the Duke of Cumberland, the Scoundrel of Mayfair, galloped past on his old bay warhorse. That ill-defined emotion squeezed her harder, but Mayfair's most elegant, torrid, and perceptive troublemaker didn't glance her way — *a mixed blessing, that. Some days a girl could use a good long stare from a rake.*

And what was that strange, miserable sensation cutting off her breathing? If she'd felt it before, she couldn't identify it.

Controlling the stallion kept Greysteil fully occupied until His Grace and his horse were well past. Then he said, "Is this a subtle means of informing me that you shan't attend the Maynards' masked ball tonight? Nor the Holly Hall Christmas Eve ball?"

She lied again, hopefully with more conviction. "Well guessed." She'd be there, all right, but better for all concerned if Grey didn't know. At the least, he'd try to stop her; at the worst, she'd lose his regard. Just the thought of alienating her oldest friend set her heart to pounding.

"That's hardly fair." He scowled. "One moment you give me such stupendous news, and the next you withdraw?" His glance ducked aside, then rose back to meet hers with sudden quirky embarrassment. "A man deserves at least a final evening in your company."

The tightness in her chest eased, eroded away by the first real pleasure she'd felt since Clarissa's horrid revelation. Of course she should have known Grey would say something kind and "make it all better," as her mother used to say when she was a child. His compliments never flattered in the airy manner of those men who considered themselves undiscovered poets — *"Oh, your eyes are so beautiful! They shine like the stars!" "And may they forever remain as distant as stars from such hollow sentiments."* — but his compliments never failed to buoy her spirits.

Her plan, her brilliant, shocking, terrifying plan — would she truly find the nerve to see it through? She had disgraced herself, it was impossible for life to continue as if nothing had happened, and so it seemed appropriate to take that daring, dreadful step before she abandoned London, returned to the country, and lived the remainder of her life as an embittered Brightenburg-less spinster. But no matter how logical it seemed on the surface, her plan's emotional undercurrents frightened and enthralled her, leaving her trembling whether she fantasized about the best possible result or the worst.

An event from last season had supplied Fidelity with the idea — the event that had destroyed poor Emily Cross's reputation and indeed her entire future. Fidelity had witnessed it to the heartbreaking *denouement* and some-times she still awoke in the night, humiliating dreams of public disgrace echoing through her. But despite her fears, Fidelity had to admit that, before the two horrific errors which had so totally undone Emily — before its botched execution, Emily's plan had been sound and well-considered. If done properly, no one would know her, possibly not even her chosen partner for the evening. All she had to do was avoid that foolish girl's mistakes. And then... She'd at least experience *it* once.

Grey still watched her, his head angled toward her, his chin tucked, his brows a solid dark bar above green eyes wide with wonder and what looked to be hurt feelings. She'd taken too long to respond, despite his pleasing compli-ment. Her conscience prickled.

Really, would it matter so much if he knew she was somewhere in the Maynards' crush? He'd not recognize her, not if she took the precautions she'd planned, and the same discretion that would prevent Georgette and Jessica from understanding her actions would keep him uninformed, as well. If he remained none the wiser...

She swallowed. "Well..."

"Say you will. For me." Grey paused. His gaze lingered on hers and deepened, then he cleared his throat. "As a friend."

Her breath hitched and the sun's gentle warmth broke over her, raising a sudden glow. Surprising, how much the moment shook her. *Good thing he added that caveat. For a moment there it almost sounded as if...* "For such a friend, how could I refuse?" She cleared her throat in turn; she'd have to rest her voice for the evening or that dratted quaver would give her away. "But Grey, this must be the last."

"Well, you won't blame me for trying to convince you otherwise, at least?"

On his last word, the stallion plunged again, flattening his ears and slewing sideways into the track's center. Grey closed his hands, sat deeper in the saddle, and held the brute in his dancing tracks.

Suddenly the conversation felt too heavy to bear. "Why don't you gallop poor Cassius and get that energy out of his system?" Fidelity blurted out. Exactly what she needed — the quickest, least painful method of getting rid of Grey while she considered her plan further. It felt foolproof and likely was, but a single mistake on her part would make her situation infinitely worse. Just the thought twisted her insides more tightly.

Thankfully his grin flashed, not further hurt feelings. "For such a friend, how could I refuse?" Grey took his life in his hands, swapping all four reins into one fist and tipping his beaver to her. "Until tonight, Fi." He paused, his fingers unerringly sorting out the handful of leather. "Bet I'll know you, no matter what you wear."

Before she could respond — *Bet you won't!* — he loosened the reins and leaned forward with a click of his tongue. Cassius half-reared and bolted away, hooves digging into the track and slewing dirt in a broad fan. A pack of horses on the far rail shied into a tangle, the laughing dandies astride them shouting and whooping encouragement. Thankfully, Palfrey only lifted her head and plodded on, ears pricked.

More surprising was the flicker of unhappiness Fidelity felt as Cassius disappeared in the Rotten Row crowd. *Why does everyone get to have fun but me?*

Wait, was that *resentment* she felt?

* * * *

Cassius plodded beneath him, weary and finally content, and Greysteil let the reins sag on the stallion's neck, his hip bones swaying with the saddle and the horse's stride. But although his body felt loose and relaxed, his face felt tight, as if he clenched his teeth like a dog growling over a bone. For three years he'd waited, observing the longing in her eyes as she'd watched that scandalous fashion-plate scoundrel dancing with whatever young thing was the current fad. Amiable those nymphs might be, aye, and delightful, too, not to mention easy on the eyes; but they couldn't compare to the svelte, alluring Fidelity Scott.

Nobody could.

She'd fallen hard for Sylvestre Brightenburg, that useless lump of society fluff. All the cretin had had to do was strut into a room, staring around in his haughty, insufferable manner, and every female in the place swooned at his feet. As if swaggering were all that was necessary to make him important; as if pretending to be a man of class and distinction would make it so. As if projecting an assumed image of himself, rather than his degenerate reality, would make Brightenburg desirable.

Truth be told, if that had been the fluff's goal, he'd pretty much succeeded. Beautiful Fidelity Scott wasn't the only gentlewoman who yearned at Brightenburg's heels and the swooning debutantes were a copper to the dozen. Greysteil scowled. Someone needed to take that insufferable cretin to task and cut him down to a more fitting size, before one of those nymphs was hurt. Or worse. And society could only hope it wasn't already too late.

And Greysteil would cheerfully throw himself off the white cliffs of Dover before he'd let Fidelity suffer from the unthinking, selfish whims of a scoundrel, or from those of anybody else, for that matter. Even if she forgot his presence as soon as that idiot entered the room.

Well, judging from her obvious embarrassment and reading between the lines of what she hadn't admitted, she'd seen the error of her ways. She'd woken up, smelled the morning beverage, and gotten over her infatuation with the silly bugger. Now it was his turn.

Greysteil smiled, although his jaws didn't relax. He'd waited for three years. Now he could sweep Brightenburg under the proverbial carpet, like the fluff he strongly resembled, and possibly beneath a real one if the opportunity presented itself.

And he could convince Fidelity to turn her attention in a much more promising direction — his.

But to accomplish his heart's desire in a single

evening — as Prince Hamlet said, aye, there's the rub. He'd have to convince her of his sincerity, the strength of his love and the constancy of his desire, while competing for her time and attention in the crush of a masked ball. A tall order, considering he hadn't even been able to hold her eye since Brightenburg had moved to town.

What he needed was a plan and for that he needed a drink. No, a workout. He turned Cassius toward Bond Street and shook the reins. A few rounds at Gentleman Jackson's gymnasium would set him right up, then it would be time to dress for the evening.

For Fidelity.

3

Fidelity's nerve gave out at the first flash of brilliant blue silk in her boudoir's candlelight. *What was I thinking?*

"No, Mary, not that one. The—" She paused, near-panic setting her heart pounding and no backup plan ready. "The evening primrose lutestring instead."

Her lady's maid hesitated at the wardrobe's door. The blue silk in her arms shimmered in the candle-light, hints of gold flickering along the neckline. "The lutestring, miss? I thought—"

"Yes, I know." *You too, huh?* "The lutestring's so much more suitable, don't you think?"

Mary studied her but carefully didn't roll her eyes. "If you say so, miss." She turned back to the wardrobe. The blue silk vanished inside.

It's for the best. Really.

The deep yellow satin glowed like a torch as Mary laid it out on the bed. Fidelity had splurged on the material and on the delicate lace trim, on the seam-stress and the matching slippers. It was a good color

for her, emphasizing her golden brown hair and setting off her blue eyes.

*And I wore it all last season. Everyone in the West
End knows that gown and they'll know me in it.
Wasn't the point of this one final evening in town to be
someone else, just for the night? To break free and
make some lovely, atrocious memories to last the rest
of my lonely life?*

Her thoughts roiled while Mary drew the silver-
backed brush through her hair. Yes, that was
resentment she felt, and it hadn't quit squeezing her
chest since Grey's gallop away. Not that she particularly wished to emulate his riding, nor have a go at the
races. But somewhere along her life's pathway she'd
put aside the delightfully fun antics, the ones
Georgette and Jessica flaunted so shamelessly, and
instead she'd drawn on a mask of serene gentility, of
good manners and good sense and great dullness. No
wonder Mr. Brightenburg paid her no attention; she
interested him less than a well-trained horse or hound.

Everyone said a sweet temperament and proper
decorum were *de rigueur* for catching a husband.
Emphasis on *husband*. If that word was removed from
the equation... If less attention were paid to perman-
ence, more to the singular experience... If she knew
her behavior would never be attributed to her...

Well, she could wriggle as sensuously as Georgette
and have just as much fun in the process. By putting
on a physical mask for one evening, she could remove
the invisible one she'd worn for so long.

For three years she'd observed Sylvestre Brightenburg. He danced with most of the debutantes, some
of the young gentlewomen, and very few of the
spinsters over twenty-one, meaning her peers. Those
he did notice were all wealthy and beautiful, and
those who held his attention the longest all wore

evocative gowns.

Hence her investment in blue silk and a Kentish needlewoman never patronized by her set. If anyone attempted to track down her masked self, it wouldn't be through her seam-stress.

And then afterward she could retire to Kent, virtue perhaps bereft, hopes faded to rags — but with memories to sustain her. At the thought, her heart pounded even harder.

Mary swirled her mane into a loose twist on the back of her head, the same way she always did. It was a lovely hairstyle, well suited to her face, and yet...

Fidelity fidgeted. "Let's do something different tonight, Mary."

The maid paused. "With your hair, miss?" She let the strands fall through her fingers, and they collapsed into a luxuriant golden mass on Fidelity's shoulder. "What do you have in mind?"

"I don't know," Fidelity admitted. She sighed. "But something different. Remember the afternoon when we played with different hairstyles? What was the one you liked so much?"

Mary's face lit up. She separated out a lock on each side of Fidelity's face, then combed the rest of her hair up the back of her head to the top, wrapped it around itself in layered waves, and pinned it into place. The remaining locks she braided on each side, leaving a few curly strands brushing her cheeks, weaving the plaits with thin blue and yellow ribbons and pinning them into a halo that framed her face.

"There, miss. That will look divine with your mask." Mary leaned over Fidelity's shoulder and whispered into her ear. "It would look even diviner with that blue gown, too."

Fidelity shot her a look, but Mary's chin was set; she meant what she'd said. And really, the hairstyle was so different from her norm. If she wore her plainest jewelry, say tiny gold studs like those everyone owned and a simple gold chain...

"I'm right. And you know it." Mary scooped the mask from the dressing table and held it in place.

It covered all of her face, rather than just her eyes, curving around her jaw line and up her forehead to where the pinned braid provided a natural boundary. The blue silk covering looked like midnight in the flickering candlelight, and the gold trim and white pearls glinted. It was beautiful. And more than that, it changed her, the width of her face, the angle of her chin, the set of her eyes; a stranger looked back at her from the glass.

The blue silk would complete the transformation, she knew. She'd never owned a gown like it, never anything so daring, and so no one would recognize her, not even her closest friends, not even Clarissa. Its lines accented hers, designed to draw a man's eyes — designed to draw Brightenburg's.

Decision time. Did she dare?

Mary shrugged, too casual by half. "I sp'ose you could always give that gown to the Miss Alcocks. If'n you're not going to wear it, I mean."

In the glass, the stranger's eyes flashed. Oh, yes, those two would be delighted to wear her gown. And they'd get into serious trouble with some rake or other the moment one of them wore it onto the street; they'd no more discretion or discernment than that well-trained hound she'd compared herself to earlier, and that was slandering the hound—

—and if she carried out her plan, then she was no better—

Face it, m'girl. You just don't want anyone else wearing that gown, if you can't. Or won't.

Truth, that; she didn't. She'd designed it; she'd

had it sewn; it was hers and hers alone. And so the honor of wearing it should go to—

Fidelity sucked in a deep breath. It settled through her in a confident wave. Her course was set — *or would that be my corset?*

"Let's see how it looks."

* * * *

The carriage had almost reached the Maynards' town home and Georgette's eyes still hadn't returned to normal size. She shook her head slowly, staring at Fidelity — or was it her cleavage? — through the last of the sunset's golden light. "I've just never seen you looking like this, Fi. You're—"

There's the danger, right there. Fidelity's temper roiled; those careless girls could ruin her evening before it began. "The first one of you who uses my name in company gets what?"

With a gasp, Georgette slapped a hand over her mouth. "Your everlasting opprobrium."

"And no chance whatsoever to wear this gown! For the rest of your lives! I'll shred it to dust rags first!"

"I'm sorry! I didn't mean it, honestly!"

Jessica laid a hand on Georgette's heaving shoulder. "But we need to call you something. Give us a name and we won't get it wrong again."

An excellent suggestion. Fidelity only paused a moment. "Call me Diana."

The Roman goddess of the hunt; the Italian for *heavenly* or *divine*. Both of the mouths before her formed perfect Os.

It seemed a proper beginning to the evening.

4

The stir started a moment after they entered the ballroom.

Fidelity didn't notice it at first. Oh, she was aware that something untoward was going on, that the crowd rippled around her, heads turning, voices whispering; but she chalked it up to the usual general masked ball silliness and carried on with her business. A few seats remained unclaimed in the corner farthest from the musicians. Mask firmly in place, she led the girls through the crowd in that direction.

Georgette whined. "Not there, F— Diana."

Fidelity glared; Georgette's glance back was innocence itself. She leaned closer and whispered, "I didn't say it. And not over in that dull corner. We'd have a much more entertaining evening here, with our friends."

"Absolutely," Jessica said. "The fun crowd."

That sounded dangerous, and a glance at the "fun crowd" confirmed the suspicion. Several older girls, their fashionable gowns hovering on the accidental verge of decency — rather like hers — gathered behind decorated fans, already surrounded by a crowd of attentive dandies. One man glanced in their direction, his plain black mask shining in the candlelight, a sharp contrast against his pale hair; then he elbowed the man beside him. Within seconds, the entire male pack stared at her, more than one jaw hanging open.

"Please," Georgette wheedled.

"Absolutely not." Fidelity turned away and continued the trek to the far corner. Tonight was not the night for those silly girls to join her in ruination or even cause an embarrassing incident. It was her night to create some discreetly indiscreet memories once Georgette and Jessica were innocently distracted, and the "fun crowd" wouldn't be much help there. *Quite the opposite, in fact.*

But within steps she realized that young pack weren't the only ones staring. Everywhere she looked, her gaze crossed someone else's — two men at the refreshment table, several older ones near the door to the card room, a legion of redcoats beside the musicians' dais, a gentleman in a deep blue tailcoat by the stairs. It seemed every man in the ballroom — and there were many many men in the ballroom — it seemed all of them stared at her.

That ripple of motion when they'd entered, those whispers she'd heard at the edge of her awareness but hadn't paid attention to... It had to be the blue silk gown. *Don't be silly; of course it's the gown. Wasn't that the entire point?*

But with the thought, a flutter began in her belly and rippled up her back, dithering through her various parts and bringing lightheaded heat to her face. For so many years she'd been — well, not precisely ignored, but not valued, either. Not sought out by the opposite sex, in all honesty. At some balls she'd enjoyed partners for every dance, but not at all of them, not by far. This sudden flood of attention drove all the air from her lungs and left her breathless, delightfully so.

Jessica leaned closer on her other side. "Do you see...?"

"Shh," Fidelity said. She looped one arm through Jessica's, the other through Georgette's, and lead them to the far corner, her steps gliding and a small smile on her lips.

Please, Lord, don't let me trip. Or stumble. Or bobble. Or...

* * * *

She was stunning. And Greysteil was appropriately stunned.

He'd taken up a stance by the staircase, feeling silly in his new navy blue swallowtail coat — he should have worn his old black Melton, he'd have been much more comfortable, and instead he'd be worrying all night if this ridiculous thing fit him properly. He always felt that way in a new coat, no matter how well it looked in the tailor's glass. But as soon as the glistening golden-haired beauty in the blue gown swept into the ballroom, he'd forgotten his wardrobe and stared.

It was her. He couldn't be fooled, no matter how that mask altered the lines of her face. Her step, her grace, the flash of gold from her upswept hair — so different from her normal style — the way she took command of the two girls in her train... no, Fidelity Scott couldn't be hidden from him, no matter how extraordinary her simple disguise.

And that gown! The silk fitted her upper body, outlining her luscious form in celestial blue the color of a darkening night sky, and the skirt clung to her legs as she walked. Swirling in front, kicking out behind her, it never quite gave him a clear image of her limbs hidden beneath the silk, just teasing moments of sudden clarity, followed too quickly by a flowing formlessness. It was the most exquisite torture he'd ever known, and he knew he'd never get enough of that torture to satisfy him.

Ripples of attention followed her path, heads turning, whispers trailing behind. But she didn't pause again. Georgette wearing primrose on Fidelity's left arm, Jessica in puce on her right — the two girls weren't nearly as well disguised — arm in arm, the three swept through the throng to a nearby cluster of chairs. Well-chosen strategic location, that; the girls wouldn't be able to slip away, at least not through the garden door.

"Who on earth...?"

Greysteil glanced over his shoulder. A masked couple stood nearby, staring at the passing beauty. The woman had to be Lady Gower; unless she wore a wig or a full turban, there was no hiding her shining silver hair.

The man shook his head. "No idea," he said a rich baritone. It sounded like Colonel Danning. "Are those the McTaggart and de Lisle girls with her?"

Mentally Greysteil shook his head; nope, not Lysandra McTaggart and Violetta de Lisle, although there were some outward similarities.

"Perhaps." Lady Gower smiled, predatory as ever. "We must find out who she is."

And ensure her identification is whispered to every broadsheet in town. Any fool could see where that was headed.

The other voices in the ballroom, the whispers surrounding them, sounded no less excited or curious, and no more certain. Judging by the reaction, no one else seemed to have penetrated Fidelity's disguise. Only he recognized her.

A simple disguise, yes. But an amazingly complete one. Everything she'd been able to alter had been — her hairstyle, her wardrobe, her jewelry, her slippers. Why on earth had she taken such pains, especially since she intended leaving town as soon as he quit pestering her?

Grey's heart stilled within him, then resumed beating, too hard, too fast. Last season Emily Cross, an ill-advised young lady possessed of more *amour* than wisdom, had contrived a disguise as complete for the Foresters' Mid-Summer's Eve ball. During the evening Emily had disappeared from the common view, only to return a half-hour later with a glowing smile, a dreamy expression, her mask dangling from her neck by its ribbons, and a grass-green stain running from her white gown's back neckline to her bum. The full description and delicious details had made almost all the gossip sheets and the poor woman had escaped to the country within days.

If Fidelity intended an amorous fling, she would never lose the mask.

Surely not. Surely his sudden worry was based upon nothing more than his own overwrought anxieties. Fidelity embodied higher standards than that; she had more discretion, more wisdom. If she sought an adventure—

Well, in all honesty, he wasn't certain what she'd do. She'd changed since Brightenburg had moved to town, become quieter, more introspective, more reserved and intensely private with her true thoughts and feelings. While he believed she'd not make a laughingstock of herself, the nagging worry niggling at his thoughts refused to be subdued.

No. No, he'd not think the worst of the situation, nor of her. Not immediately. He'd wait and watch and let her game play out. But the possibility only intensified his determination; he'd play his game, too.

And he'd not consider for a moment who she might have decided to play her game *with*.

Getting close to her in that crush was going to be a nightmare. But as she glided into a corner near the statuary and potted plants, as she turned and surveyed the crowd, the strength of the yearning that swept through him insisted it would be a worthy battle.

Because she was all he wanted, his only prize.

* * * *

Sylvestre Brightenburg nearly choked on his champagne. He couldn't rip his stare from the Aphrodite who'd just crossed the ballroom, that ravishing and ravishable vision now standing by the potted plants as if guarding the door to the rear gardens. The two young ladies hanging on her arms were desperately ordinary in comparison — one in yellow, the other in pink, one's hair darker, both wearing curls and ribbons; nothing he hadn't seen, danced with, possessed, tossed away when they'd tired him. Sooner or later, they always tired him.

But this one, oh, she was magnificent. The proud lift of her chin, her graceful carriage, the businesslike stride combined with that fascinating sway, the generous gifts of her figure, softened but not disguised by the glorious blue silk — it was more than a man could stand. And if she hadn't wanted his attention, all of his attention, then she shouldn't have worn that gown.

He had to meet her and then she'd be his, for the

evening, at least. And that was all he needed. Without a second thought, he pushed his way through the crowd.

* * * *

They converged on her from either side, two tall men behind simple black half-masks, the one wearing the blue tailcoat who'd earlier stood by the stairs and watched her trek across the ballroom, and Sylvestre Brightenburg. To the rest of the crowd, he might be anonymous, identifiable behind the mask only by black hair, hazel eyes, silk stockings, white breeches, and a stylish maroon swallowtail. To everyone else, he could only be a cipher. But he could never be hidden from Fidelity, and his swaggering approach through the ballroom's flowing crowd hitched her breath in her throat.

His swaggering approach, aye. And his legs. Don't forget those legs. Give the girl credit; Georgette had a point regarding what he does to silk stockings and breeches.

Both men paused at a polite distance and bowed. Both moved with exceptional grace; both demanded her attention by their very presence. And both spoke at once.

"Might I have—"

Blue Tailcoat broke off, his voice abandoning the impromptu and unintended duet, one strong hand rising and pushing his thick, dark forelock from his face. Something in the sudden movement spoke, not of indecision, but of an abrupt change of plans. Fidelity couldn't be certain, for the moment lasted less than a second, and Brightenburg's rich tenor didn't pause.

"—the first dance?" He finished the sentence alone.

Gracious. The pounding sound she heard was her pulse, rising in her ears and skipping faster against the rustling of the surrounding crowd.

He'd noticed her. The blue gown had done its job within moments of her entrance. Sylvestre Brightenburg had noticed her and asked her to dance.

Fidelity started to blurt out the only possible answer she could return. But a motion on her right made her pause. Blue Tailcoat shifted from one foot to the other. His broad shoulders slumped and the scowl he shot in Brightenburg's direction could only be called vexed.

"Exactly what I'd intended to say," he said.

Blue Tailcoat. A mundane nickname for an elegant man, with his blunt jaw and well-fitting evening clothes, clear green eyes and thick dark hair. She might need a more appropriate moniker for him. Actually, she had the distinct feeling she should recognize him; a strange flavor of familiarity hung between them, as if his name tickled at the tip of her tongue but refused to stammer forth.

Even in the depths of her Brightenburg-induced giddiness, she wouldn't be rude. She smiled at Blue Tailcoat. "Perhaps the second?"

Brightenburg's turn to scowl. Even more thrilling; he disliked having competition. *Terrible behavior for a gentlewoman, but oh, how delicious!*

Blue Tailcoat's answering smile was lopsided, good-natured, and totally charming. A tide of gentle warmth flowed beneath her giddiness. He said, "I shall await your return with bated breath."

And then somehow her arm was through the crook of Brightenburg's elbow and he'd whisked her away to join the lengthening line for the first dance.

5

"Will you give me your name?"

Brightenburg's smile gleamed in the candlelight, somewhere between dazzling and downright wicked. Red and gold highlights glinted in his dark hair, reflected in the satin of his mask, flowed down his shoulders and chest along the maroon wool, tapering into shadows at his waist, and below that—

Fidelity jerked her gaze up. From across the line he watched her watching him, full lips pulled into a sideways smirk. *His lips on hers...* what would it be like? Did she dare find out tonight? He looked willing. Actually, he looked like Adonis, awaiting her exploring fingers; like Icarus, blazing and bright before his fall. The music started, a lively tune, and somewhere to her right movement began as the first couple, whoever they were, initiated the dance.

She'd waited so long for a night of her own. The reality was everything she'd dreamed of while hidden away in her boudoir — everything and more. Those weren't imaginary toes curling, and if her heart pitter-pattered any faster, it would take off from out of her chest like a startled hummingbird.

She looked away, sucked in a steadying breath, and stepped sideways with the group, advancing along the dance's line. "My name? Correct me if I'm wrong, but wouldn't that defeat the entire purpose of a masked ball?"

His eyebrows quirked in a humorous arch. "What good can come of not knowing one's partner?"

The leading couple danced down the line — of course, the Maynards' niece, Brenda, skipping along arm in arm with Mr. Culver. It wasn't the first time the two had opened a ball together, but for some reason, the poor girl seemed pleased with her choice, glowing with delight as she approached then swishing past in a flash of icy muslin. In the line opposite, Brightenburg's gaze followed the couple's path, eyeing the girl's backside — his target was impossible to miss — and tracing down toward the pale skin of her ankles, visible beneath her hemline as her skirts flared around her.

Fidelity's fluttery excitement stilled, leaving her surprised and a trifle hurt. Willing, aye, he certainly seemed *that*. Granted, Belinda Maynard was a pretty girl and reportedly sweet-natured; her dowry was not inconsiderable. But a truly well-bred gentleman would reserve such attentions for his partner.

Brightenburg swung back around. His eyes had narrowed, his lip curled; he'd enjoyed the view, in a very basic way. Fidelity stifled a snort. *Basic, indeed.* And with her oh-so-brilliant plan, who was she to find fault?

That curled lip was entirely too roguish. She looked away and pretended not to notice his slight. The dancers swirled around her. Satins and silks flashed in the chandeliers' blaze, delicate lace forming pale accents, flowers providing bright ones. The gentlemen's maroons, deep blues, and sober blacks strengthened the line. Several dancers wore that new green silk everyone was raving about; she'd nearly bought it instead of the celestial blue, but the extra expense had been fearful. It was beautiful, though.

Partway down the line, a familiar and charming smile caught her eye. Blue Tailcoat chatted with a young lady in primrose yellow, and Fidelity blinked before she recognized Georgette, demure and delightful behind her half-mask. The change from the hoyden who'd helped terrorize the morning room last week was astounding. Perhaps there was hope for that girl yet. *Well... perhaps.*

Still not their turn. With so many couples in the line, the dance could last ten minutes or more. Fidelity folded her hands and didn't bother to hide her smug little smile. Ten minutes with Sylvestre Brightenburg was no punish-ment.

Even if his eye tended to wander. She'd noticed that tendency in him before; why hadn't she been prepared to endure it?

He cleared his throat. "If admiration grows between us, wouldn't it be preferable if we could find each other after the evening's entertainment is past? And if we decide our personalities and tastes don't suit, wouldn't it be better if we knew to avoid each other's company?"

"Oh, but there's excitement in mystery." Her moment of satisfaction had softened the sting of his slight, and her voice held steady. Of course he hadn't hurt her on purpose, and hadn't she been thrilled mere minutes ago for having any of Sylvestre Brightenburg's attention, any at all? "Wouldn't it be better to allow our mutual admiration or otherwise to grow without interference from prior assumptions? Perish the thought, but if I'd previously formed a dislike for the cut of your jib—" *as if that were possible* — "then a few hours of mystery now might go far to change that opinion."

He scowled. *So quickly his mood changes.* "At least tell me your residence." No gruffness in his tone, nor wheedling, but a firmness that spoke of determination. "St. James's Square, I'll be bound. You've the air and deportment of a duchess."

The pounding of her heart intensified. She'd thought their bantering a game, but his scowl gave her pause. He was serious, determined to learn her identity, and her thrill deepened, shivering her from hair to slippers.

Sylvestre Brightenburg, London's *beau* to end all *beaux*, intended to peer beneath her mask.

Excellent.

"And the gown," he added, his glance roving over her and lingering at her bosom. "That's the gown of a noblewoman, to be sure."

Only his gaze touched her, but it scorched like a physical flame. Fidelity tingled, all too aware of his nearness, his strength, his heat, and the tingling rippled out from her center to places she didn't normally think about while in company. If he could cause such exquisite sensations with only a look, what of his lips? his hands? his...

And still he stared. The need to squirm rose within her, tempering the lovely tingling and tamping her internal fire down to a dim glow. That was altogether too long and too intimate a stare for such a gathering. If witnessed, tongues would begin wagging: *Sylvestre Brightenburg's got his eye on that wench in blue, the one in the shameless dress. Who is she?* And surely everyone in the ballroom was already transfixed by the spectacle of Brightenburg making a spectacle of her. No need to look; she could feel their stares, just as she felt his.

No, catching the public fancy would spoil everything. She'd be watched, hounded, followed home, and she'd never be able to slip away from the ballroom unobserved, the most crucial step in executing her plan without ruining herself the rest of the way. (*Was it possible to be just a little bit ruined? Curious thought.*) A chance to retire to somewhere more private with *a certain gentleman* would never present itself if the entire crowd watched her, and her evening's effort would be wasted.

Because she'd never work up the nerve to try her brilliant plan a second time.

Fidelity turned sideways, giving Brightenburg a good view of her shoulder, and peered back along the line. Georgette still stood in position, her smile mischievous but at least not outrageously so, and Blue Tailcoat seemed charmed as well as charming. Fidelity kept looking. A pale pink gown two positions further along, another pale pink past the emerald silk, more pale pink toward the end — but no deep puce, the shade of a dusky rose. No Jessica. Not good.

The music lifted and it was finally their turn. She advanced to meet Brightenburg, almost to kissing distance — *far too warm in this ballroom; what on earth were the Maynards thinking with that massive fire?* — then they retreated back to the line, cut behind their waiting neighbors in a round robin, traded places with them, advanced again. Her feet and body performed without her conscious assistance, her attention mesmerized by the gold flecks in Brightenburg's eyes. Admiring him was delightful; dancing with him was electrifying. His every step hit the beat precisely — *if only mine did* — and his grace made her feel clumsy in comparison.

Still he stared at her, his lip curling again. What

on earth was he seeing in her expression that riveted him so? Whatever it was, the thought of him reading her secret intentions so clearly sent said intentions scurrying for shelter, to somewhere deep within her, and she quailed. Her heart pounded, and not only with the exercise. No, she couldn't go through with it. Yes, she could. No—

His arms entwined with hers, breaking her ridiculous roundabout of indecision, and they turned, skipping together between the lines toward the far end. That lovely heat began again, centered beneath his forearm where it pressed against her stomach, far too intimate a touch and not at all proper, no matter how much her decadent half enjoyed it. Oh, this wasn't working out at all as she'd planned. Those eyes, encircling them around the ballroom — they followed her every motion, catalogued his every flirtation. Witnesses; far far too many witnesses for her to slip away.

Frantic for a diversion, Fidelity again scanned the ballroom as they danced along, the deep colors of the men's attire flashing past on one side, the pale and brilliant shades of the women's on the other. A gentleman wearing a sober black Melton coat and a plain black mask stood near the doors to the card room, chatting with Mrs. Maynard. The coat looked rather like Grey's, but the man himself wasn't quite... too tall, too stocky? Or was she merely misjudging the perspective? It was the closest she'd seen to Grey's disreputable old coat, the one he wore nearly everywhere, and yet she couldn't convince herself it was he.

Frowning, she kept looking. No puce gowns along the front half of the line. None near the musicians' dais or the refreshment area. Thank-fully, none near the fun crowd, thanks be for small blessings.

At the line's end they separated, his fingers

sliding through hers and brushing her hip in passing. She rounded Brenda Maynard, still smiling and with a damp glow tugging the curl from her bangs, and then Fidelity danced back behind the distaff line. Not near the stairs, nor at the entrance to the card room—

There. Closing in on the door to the gardens, a dusky rose gown, walking far too close beside a tall masculine form decked out in those dandified formal trousers Beau Brummell wore to such effect. Any young man wearing those was automatically not a suitable companion for one of her cousins, certainly not outside among the heady scents of the slumbering earth, and most certainly not without a chaperone.

And the behavior she expected from her young nieces had no bearing whatsoever on the behavior she couldn't decide whether to expect from herself.

Without pausing, Fidelity danced right past her place in line. Ducking her chin, she eased to a gliding walk, slid through the crowd of watchers, ignored the increasing whispers and turning heads, wended her way between bodies toward the far corner at the fastest pace she dared, and cut her niece and Trousers off at the door.

"And precisely where do you think you're going, young lady?"

Jessica's ribbons bobbed as she jumped. "F— for pity's sake, *Diana*, you startled me."

Trousers released Jessica's arm as if she'd electrified him. His red mask flared in the candlelight, a strong masculine statement, but his guilty grin spoke more of a schoolroom too recently left.

"You most certainly weren't intending to wander the gardens this evening, were you? *Without a chaperone?*" She glared at Trousers with serious and violent intent. With all their fascinated witnesses, she'd better hope nothing happened to him that night. No barrister would ever be able to get her off, lightly or otherwise, should he take a tumble in front of a runaway carriage or anything.

Perhaps her glare said all that needed saying. Or at least Trousers backed away, tossing Jessica a rueful glance. Two more steps, and he vanished into the crush.

The little minx's lips pushed out in a pouting moue. Her ribbons, curling in delicate pink and white spirals near her right ear, bobbed again as she shook herself. "Look me in the eye and tell me you wouldn't do the same if it were Sylvestre Brightenburg on your arm."

Fidelity rocked back, her heart thudding. Of course she wouldn't do such a thing... except she'd intended doing precisely that. And worse.

A glint appeared in Jessica's eyes. The pout gave way to a scowl. "You would, wouldn't you... *Diana?*"

Fidelity froze. Or perhaps the ballroom froze around her; it was difficult to tell. Shocked to her core, she could only stare at the minx and dream lovely dreams of the polished hardwood floor opening beneath her and sucking her out of the moment. But before she could sort her wistful fantasy from reality, a big, luscious shape loomed in her peripheral vision and a mellow tenor voice spoke.

"Diana, is it?"

Oh, no. For the first time in her life, Fidelity wished for some stronger words.

Brightenburg slid between two potted plants and eased closer. High color flushed his cheeks and the golden flecks in his eyes had darkened with anger. His lip's curl had tightened, but something that looked remarkably like satisfaction chased the rest of his anger from his face. He leaned over her, far more near than could possibly be countenanced by polite society, and his gentle touch squeezed her elbow.

"Diana, my dear, you *left* the *dance.*"

And if she explained why, she'd ruin Jessica's reputation, before Jessica had another opportunity to do so for herself. *Think, think; what to say?* Fidelity shot a glare at the willful cause of her current dilemma. She might as well have glared at the moon; Jessica's eyes resembled innocent blue saucers, fixated on Brightenburg as if pinned there. And if the silly girl didn't breathe soon, she really would swoon.

With a three-note swirl, the music ended, and scattered applause rippled through the crowd. The first dance, the all-important opening to the ball, was over. Her ten minutes with Sylvestre Brightenburg, which could have led to more as the evening progressed, instead had been squandered chasing down Jessica and doing the job her aunt, the wretched girl's mother, refused to do. Fidelity gritted her teeth. It was past time to take the chit in hand.

A discreet pinch, harder than it perhaps needed to be, and Jessica started from her trance with a gasp. "Ouch! That wasn't—"

Fidelity cleared her throat and lowered her chin. Jessica's mouth snapped closed. The petulance returned to her pout and for a moment, guilt joined it; the minx realized what she'd interrupted.

But only for a moment. *Too much to ask, that.*

"What, are you hurt?" Brightenburg asked. A puzzled line creased his forehead.

"Oh, no—"

"Oh, yes," Fidelity said at the same time. She awarded Brightenburg her sweetest false smile. "Would you excuse us, please?" Without awaiting a reply, she slid her arm around Jessica's and tugged.

Jessica scowled but dropped her voice to a whisper as she followed along. "Tell me you wouldn't do the same—"

A harder tug, and she fell silent. But just as Fidelity could feel the covertly watching eyes, she could feel the resentment broiling within Jessica. Hopefully the connection worked both ways; hopefully Jessica could equally feel the resentment broiling within her.

She tugged Jessica to the sitting area, as far from listening ears as she could manage. "Plop your anatomy down upon that chair and remain there for the next two dances."

A startled, gurgling sort of noise responded. "This is a *ball—*"

"And if you give me any grief, you'll accompany me in a few days' time when I return to the country."

The yank as Jessica tugged her arm from their *faux* cousinly entanglement sent Fidelity into a stumbling sidestep. She glared. Jessica glared back, color rising in her cheeks.

"You wouldn't."

Fidelity let her pointed silence speak for her.

The flush darkening Jessica's round cheeks faded to a furious and bloodless alabaster. Her voice dropped to a murmur, barely audible beneath the ballroom's ruckus. "Fi, you can't. We need you here, in town."

Oh, and she would play that card. Duty, duty, always duty, and never a chance for *her.* Fidelity had had enough. "So much for you ever wearing this dress—"

"We aren't in company, so that doesn't count." Jessica waved at the surrounding crush, too noisy and distant for their *sotto voce* conversation to be overheard. "Besides, if you leave for the country, what does it matter? We'll be stuck at home, never able to go out. What use would I have for your dress or any other?"

"It's time for your mother to resume her responsibilities."

Jessica scoffed. "She'll never come to town."

"She must, because I'm not your mother. Overseeing your coming out is something she must do herself. Now go sit down or be ready to leave town in two days' time."

Fury flashed in those blue eyes, artless no more. "I thought you were our friend. I thought you were someone we could depend on. But you're just like Mama — too busy with your own concerns to bother yourself with us. I hate you!" Jessica thrust past her and stalked away through the crowd.

Before Fidelity could draw even a breath, a touch on her arm drew her around. Georgette studied her with her usual innocence, but her slackened jaw spoke of uncertainty. Great; she'd heard at least part of that exchange. Behind her, Blue Tailcoat's charming smile seemed a tad fixed. He hadn't overheard, but the argumentative atmosphere couldn't have been missed. Beyond his shoulder, heads finally began to swivel away from their tableau.

"Is — everything all right?" Georgette asked.

Was anything? "Of course. Jessica's merely tired and needs to rest a few minutes." Hopefully that would make the situation clear.

From the way Georgette's already wide eyes widened further, it did nothing of the sort. Granted, the thought of Jessica ever being tired was rather ludicrous, especially as she hadn't danced yet.

The first strains of the next tune sang above the crowd's rumbles. Great; something slow and gliding, just when she could use a wild country dance to work off some nervous energy.

"My dance, I believe." A hint of possession seeped into Blue Tailcoat's smile.

Fidelity's heart skipped up toward her throat, startling here, and a strange eagerness filled her. *Down, girl.* She opened her mouth to accept—

"No." Again a lusciously masculine form loomed beside her, and she had to hide a little jump of surprise. *How can such a large man approach so quietly?* But behind his black half-mask, Brightenburg scowled. "The lady didn't finish her dance with me, so I claim this one, as well."

Blue Tailcoat lowered his blunt chin, meeting Brightenburg's glower with coolness. "You know, it's the lady's prerogative—"

Brightenburg shook his head like a bear. "I insist."

And in the action, no mercy showed, nor understanding. The scowl deepened across his expression and his eyes slitted. He'd have his dance or the entire ballroom would learn why not.

Fidelity's blood chilled. *No, no, everything was going wrong.*

But before she could finish panicking, Blue Tailcoat bowed. "Unlike some, I consider it exceptionally poor manners indeed to embarrass or inconvenience a lady. Very well." The coolness in his eyes solidified to clear green ice. "But this discussion is not over."

"Are you calling me out?" Brightenburg's laugh rumbled beneath the whispers surrounding them. "I look forward to it. Come, *Diana.*"

Again he took her arm and led her away. But not before she saw the startled, disbelieving expression on Blue Tailcoat's face.

6

Flattering. Yes, it was flattering that Brightenburg, the most luscious man in Mayfair, insisted
upon completing their dance. Fidelity reminded herself of that, forced the thought to the forefront of her
mind.

And tried to force out the irritation she really felt.

The lines advanced in step, retreated, then broke
into squares of two couples. Fidelity glided into place,
a half-step behind Brightenburg's precision, and
turned to face the center, her partner diagonally
across, another couple to her right and left at oppos-
ing corners. Their half-masks prevented her from
recognizing them, but their open, fascinated stares
were sufficiently mortifying; if they turned out to be
members of her set, she'd never leave Kent again. The
music purred along, maddeningly slow, as they joined
hands and glided around in a sort of maypole circle.

No matter how she tried to shrug it off, she
couldn't help but feel put out by the little contre-
temps. Which was silly, of course; she'd already

decided she should be flattered by his attention, no matter how it had been forced upon her. The squares of dancers dissolved into arm-in-arm couples, reforming the line, but Fidelity again found herself half a step behind. If only she had the musical sense of a tortoise. She hurried to catch up—

—and Brightenburg grabbed her hand and yanked her into position, much as she'd yanked at Jessica's arm minutes ago.

Fidelity stumbled into place, too shocked to resist, and cold realization flooded her. She didn't feel flattered because he had no intention of flattering her. There was no compliment in his manner, no attention worth the having. No, she'd offended him, and he wanted her and the rest of the crowd to know it.

How ruddy rude.

"So why did you leave the dance, *Diana?*"

If he put any more emphasis on her false name, he'd wear it out. Which would be a pity, for she'd just assumed it.

Calm, serene, unflappable. Easy to appreciate and love — desperately she repeated her usual soothing chant, but wisps of anger slid past her defenses and the coldness in her chest deepened. Rude. Not brusque, not merely demanding, but rude. He'd been more rude than the most jaundiced rake, the saltiest sailor, the most villainous highwayman. At the evening's start, she'd been ready to abandon her virtue for the man. And he'd returned nothing but slights and rudeness.

So much for Brightenburg's company being no punishment. She'd yearned for his attention for such an achingly long time, but now that she had it, she couldn't say she valued it.

And from this new perspective, his earlier question carried a different and disturbing meaning. "*Will you give me your name?"* he'd asked at the first dance's opening. At least, those had been his words. But what he'd meant was, *Will you give me control over you?* For if he'd learned her identity...

No, she wouldn't do it. She'd not give him her name nor her virtue, not after such appalling behavior on his part. And the relief that swept through her at the decision was both a surprise and, in itself, another relief. She could expect proper propriety from her cousins without a blush for herself.

And in her turn, she had no intention of telling him the truth. Jessica might be determined to ruin herself, but Fidelity refused to assist. But she had to tell him something — *why did you leave the dance, Diana?* — or he'd become even more unbearable. Thankfully, she needn't think hard for a believable white lie.

"I'd just realized that young whippersnapper was in attendance — you know, the one in the red half-mask? — and I won't allow my — my *nieces* to keep such company." Quick catch, that; if she'd admitted the girls were her cousins, she'd have given him a clue in the hunt he surely intended to mount after the ball. Behind her mask, she allowed herself a smile. "I do apologize, but it seemed best to warn him off before he made a nuisance of himself."

Again the lines faded into squares. Again they joined hands, glided in a circle, and returned to position.

And again he laughed. But a brittleness in his tone hinted he didn't believe her. "You mean Tate the younger? Oh, aye, I can certainly see where you'd be concerned about *him*." He lowered his voice as they stepped close together and began their own, private circle. "He's purely savage, he is, at the ripe age of sixteen."

Tate the younger? The painfully shy, polite, studious younger son of the Earl of Danvers? Heat swept into Fidelity's face. Perhaps she hadn't chosen her fictitious villain all that well, even if he had been leading Jessica into the back garden when caught. Or maybe Jessica had been leading him. He'd certainly let go of her arm fast enough.

Whoever had been at fault, Fidelity's lie was apparent and there was nothing she could do except bluster it out. "My dear sir, if you had the guidance of two young and mischievous nieces, even for a single evening, believe me, you wouldn't ignore the sinful potential in such a handsome young man, either."

His eyes narrowed. No, he didn't believe her. "Sinful." He drawled out the word as if tasting it, waited for her to advance with the dance, then repeated it at a whisper, inches from her face. "Sinful. You'd know something of that, wouldn't you, Diana... it's Marchmont, is it not?"

It took her a few measures to understand his question, and a few measures more, as she turned away and circled with her neighbor's partner, to restrain her laughter. Oh, that was rich — he thought her Diana Marchmont, the elegant, proud, *married* Duchess of Benhall, out for a romp with a commoner! *How wrong can a man be?*

And more interestingly, what will happen if he ever confronts the real Duchess of Benhall and the duke hears of it?

The lines of dancers flowed back together as she carefully wiped the hilarity from her expression; her face might be hidden behind the mask, but her eyes weren't. Considering his overbearing behavior, it seemed best to let Brightenburg's incorrect assumption stand. After the ball, he'd go off on a wildly inappropriate tangent in his hunt for her. The Duchess of

Benhall, needless to say, faced no danger, with her
battalion of footmen and servants. Not to mention her
wealthy and powerful husband.

For a moment indecision unsettled her. Perhaps
she'd merely become too content with gentle, attentive
manners — like Grey's; he'd never behave in such a
boorish manner. Granted, one couldn't expect a wild
mustang stallion to show the elegance of a Thoroughbred... Grey had promised he'd be in attendance. Had
that truly been his sober old black Melton coat she'd
seen? There was something to be said for manners,
and she peered down the line to the corner where he'd
stood earlier. But the redcoats had flooded the area
and the black Melton was gone.

She took a deep breath and straightened. Again
Brightenburg stared at her from his place in the men's
line, his gaze lingering on her bosom and tracing down
her body. She hid a shiver, but this time, his too-bold
attention aroused her self-consciousness, not that
delicious tingling, the one she'd reveled in before.
Strange, that. His invisible touch still traced over her
skin beneath the cerulean silk, as strong and sure as
his hand could have been. The change wasn't in his
behavior, but in her response.

A change in the tempo; a shifting in the lines.
The music was ending, her ten minutes with Sylvestre
Brightenburg — her second ten minutes — were well
and truly over, and if she felt any disappointment, it
was too deep for her to notice.

She turned with the other dancers and applauded
the musicians, ignoring Brightenburg's scowl.

As he reached for her arm, she withdrew it, then
settled her hand demurely atop his crooked elbow.
Blue Tailcoat had reminded her that ladies had the
prerogative and she intended to exercise hers,
particularly while those surreptitious glances followed

her every movement. At least stares had quit tracing her steps; that was a minor victory, right there.

Brightenburg's scowl deepened; he'd had other plans and didn't like it when she foiled them. Well, he'd simply have to bear his disappointment, and she walked silently beside him back to her chair, her side blessedly free from his heat.

Jessica still slouched in her punishment, one crossed foot swaying to currently nonexistent music in jerky little swings. Her pout seemed permanently engraved across her features, blue eyes sulky, but she sat up straight, more like a young gentlewoman, when her glance met Fidelity's across the ballroom. Best to pretend she hadn't noticed anything; a full-out war with Jessica was the last thing Fidelity wanted to cap the evening.

Beside Jessica's chair, Blue Tailcoat waited patiently, hands clasped at his back. Something about Fidelity's approach drew a deep smile from him, more intense than the charming one he'd given Georgette during the first dance. Behind his black half-mask, green eyes flashed a clear fire. Her pulse quickened again. She couldn't say she disliked Blue Tailcoat's subtle flirtations, no matter how strongly she'd withdrawn from Brightenburg's not-so-subtle ones. And Blue Tailcoat truly had a charming smile. Whoever he was; surely she should recognize him, even behind the mask. Was he perhaps one of the gentlemen sharing rooms on Seamore Place? Caird, Ponsonby, Crompton? They were all a few years younger than she, but nevertheless delightful gentlemen.

He bowed for her. "My dance, I believe." His voice deepened, quickening her pulse again. And the snubbing shoulder he turned to Brightenburg meant he intended to claim her hand, no matter what objections might be thrown this time.

And thrown they were.

"Indeed, no," Brightenburg said. His too-loud voice rang above the crowd's rumble. *"Diana —* the lady you insist upon importuning — just finished a difficult dance. She must be given time to rest, and I," he bowed over her hand, "will fetch ices for her and her lovely companions."

Fidelity froze. Heads began turning their way again, eyes openly peering between bodies and taking note. *Just when everything seemed to be settling down...* Strange that she'd never before noted Brightenburg's boorishness; it seemed to be an ingrained habit of his and if so, she should have witnessed it years ago.

And then she'd not have wasted the time on him.

Color flowed up from Blue Tailcoat's collar, darkening his face. But the anger didn't tint his voice. "The lady must be permitted to decide for herself. Madame, would you prefer to rest or dance?"

At the clear put-down, Jessica's mouth formed a perfect O. Her eyes did, too, astonishment personified, and she glanced aside at Brightenburg as if eager to witness some violent response. Embarrassing behavior, but hopefully it was a lesson learned.

Just as it is for me. All that glitters is not gold, nor even attractive at closer sight. And at the thought, a sense of freedom, of relief and delight, relaxed her muscles. Whatever came after sloughing off years of infatuation, she was ready for it.

The opening measures for the next rang through the ballroom, lively and inviting. Fidelity's feet and bottled-up nervous energy made the decision for her. *"Miss Moore's Rant!"* she said. "Oh, let's dance!" Without thinking, she turned toward the floor, one hand reaching for her new partner. His arm slid beneath her fingers as he met her halfway, a wide grin splitting his face.

Too late, she remembered Brightenburg. She hadn't approved of his behavior and couldn't say she'd enjoyed their second dance — but rudeness on his part was no excuse for rudeness on hers. But when she swung back around, an answering flush had reached his hairline.

Her heart fell to her slippers. Too late to save the situation. All she could do was hope he'd cause no further scandal.

"Excuse me," she said. "Your offer is very kind, but I do prefer to dance."

Brightenburg whirled and shoved his way into the crush, vanishing between a feathered headdress and a turban.

* * * *

Brightenburg paused behind the sheltering screen of potted plants and fumed. Impossible to believe such a stunningly beautiful woman would actually be interested in that milksop after dancing with a *real* man. She was too much a woman for that Molly-ish behavior, all curves and fire and hidden passion. From the challenging expression she'd worn when he'd first approached her, she sought an adventure, and he was the proper man to give her one.

Impossible it was to believe, but there she went, her hand on the milksop's elbow, not even glancing back at *him*. Not sparing him further attention, as if the possibilities — the skin-flushing, spine-tingling, amorous possibilities — weren't worth her considera-tion.

She'd turned him on, aroused him to his core, and then walked away with a lesser man. She'd flirted, holding forth rather than answer-ing his questions straight out — and now *she walked away.*

He'd thought more highly of Diana Marchmont than that. Everyone knew her husband, older as he was, didn't — *couldn't* — do her justice. But there she went. A tease, she was. A flirt, and deserved what was coming to her — and someday, someday soon, he'd see that she got it.

In the meantime, he needed another partner. The fire flooding through him could not be contained. He'd return to her soon, but for now—

7

Blue Tailcoat eased her into position and took his place in the line opposite. At his encouraging smile, her heart lifted, if not back to its usual position within her chest, then at least to somewhere around her midriff. Yes, he was charming, and kind, willing to overlook both the indiscretions Brightenburg had rained upon her and the unthinking rudeness she'd returned. She couldn't get a second chance to start the ball, but like a true gentleman, Blue Tailcoat was perfectly willing to pretend the first start had never happened.

For that small mercy, she'd be grateful. Even as Brightenburg, the *beau* that got away, offered his arm to a glittering beauty wearing that expensive green silk. Arm in arm, they joined the line's end.

Was that Clarissa? It certainly looked like her, height, figure, casually graceful carriage, coils of auburn hair gleaming in the chandeliers' blaze. The amber cross looked like hers, too, and the simple gold chain. She'd never said she'd indulged in any green

Love, Unmasked   57

silk. Of course, Fidelity had never mentioned buying the cerulean, either.

An unwanted, startling thought stilled her in place. Clarissa had worn a new and gorgeous gown, a different hairstyle, plain and simple jewelry. Had she...? Had she too planned...? *No, surely not.*

Before she could finish the thought, the music whirled away, taking the dancers with it, and Fidelity's feet chose to follow Blue Tailcoat's lead, leaving her conjecture behind. Of course she missed the beat, and no matter how much extra energy she put into her *balancé* and *rigaudon*, as usual she couldn't catch up. Humiliating, and the heat blooming in her face gave her dead away. Even Blue Tailcoat couldn't be so charming as to miss her embarrassment.

At the first turn she reached across for his hand, fully expecting it to be waiting, waving impatiently. Instead, her fingers met empty air. A fraction later, he completed his turn, flashed her a delighted smile, and closed his fingers around hers. They turned together, again a half-beat behind, and galloped between the lines, hurrying to catch up to the music.

Her heart felt as if it would burst with gratitude. Impossible to believe that such a polished gentleman couldn't keep to the rhythm. No, he'd done that deliberately. He'd seen her tendency to fall behind and had fallen behind with her, rather than display his superiority to the watching crowd. A marvelous dancer, yes — and the sort who didn't claim the spotlight alone but who made his partner seem equally excellent.

Or who let himself look silly with her.

She answered his brilliant smile with one of her own. Then they split apart at the line's end, circling around the outside back to their places.

Brightenburg danced past with the woman who

might be Clarissa — no, no perhaps about it, only
Clarissa kicked up her heels in quite that decadent
manner. He whirled past Fidelity without even a
glance aside, his hand pressed against his new
partner's arm, his fawning, staring attention wholly
focused upon her bosom swathed in green silk. The
smooth cheeks and grim mouth beneath the woman's
matching green mask were tinged a dark pink;
Clarissa didn't seem to enjoy Brightenburg's flirtations any more than Fidelity had.

So we've both been cured. Startling thought, but
Fidelity realized it was true. If Brightenburg asked her
to dance again, she'd claim tiredness, even though
refusing him would be deliberate rudeness. More
importantly, if the opportunity to vanish with him
presented itself, she'd let it slip away. Blue Tailcoat
might not be as overbearingly virile and attractive, but
he behaved like a gentleman and wholeheartedly
joined with his partner. With him opposite her,
nothing felt forced, and she got the impression he'd
bite off his own arm before he'd yank her into
position.

Fidelity couldn't suppress her widening grin. As
the last notes drew out, as she and Blue Tailcoat flew
into place — still a half-beat behind — her heart raced
from the delightful exercise and her feet yearned for
more. But despite her yearning, the music drew to a
dignified close. Reluctantly she joined the other
dancers in applause, and halfway through, she turned
and shared her appreciation with her partner.

He beamed at her. "I don't think I've ever enjoyed
a dance so much in my life."

Unlike her, not even a tinge of sweat dampened
his face; he'd taken the vigorous exercise with aplomb,
as if he'd be comfortable dancing all night. And that
impish, inviting smile — he hadn't lost it throughout

the entire whirling-dervish dance, and it only broadened as she accepted his arm and followed his lead from the floor. Her heart fluttered. No, he wasn't Caird — not enough swagger — and not Ponsonby, either. Who on earth could he be? Surely she should know him, with or without his mask. His eyes resembled Grey's, a little, at least, but she'd seen Grey's old black Melton earlier and this couldn't be him. Besides, Blue Tailcoat didn't look at her the way Grey did, as a friend. Blue Tailcoat looked at her with something more, something she didn't quite understand.

Side by side they wended through the crowd, back toward the seating area. Fidelity peered across the ballroom, but Jessica had disappeared; well, fair enough, she'd been told to sit out two dances and those were now done. More surprising was Blue Tailcoat's behavior. She'd expected him to step out but instead he sauntered, as if unwilling to reach their destination and the conclusion of their time together. The inherent compliment made her smile again. Perhaps she should ask him to fetch her an ice, or would that be flirting?

Before she could decide, he squeezed her fingers. "I just love a masked ball. Don't you? There's something so—" his smile quirked at the edges "—so very mysterious about them, what with pretending to be someone else and leading on one's partners, and so on."

Her thoughts stuttered. He couldn't possibly have overheard her earlier conversation with Brightenburg, could he? But there was no guile in his eyes, merely the same intense delight. No, it didn't seem possible. Still she hesitated before answering. "You don't wish to discover your partner's secrets?"

Gentle pressure on her hand and his steps slowed even further. At this rate, they might never

reach the chairs. "Immediately? Where would be the
fun in that?" A shake of his head, firm but good-
natured. "For maximum enjoyment, little adventures
should be extended, explored, wallowed in like a
happy pig. They shouldn't be brushed aside as
unimportant."

That was too close for coincidence. Heat invaded
Fidelity's face, thankfully hidden by the mask. "Have
you been eavesdropping on my conversations, sir?"

"Nothing so nefarious. It's just that some—" He
broke off abruptly, as if rethinking the words he'd
intended to say. "Well, some *people* tend to repeat
themselves, using the same tired old lines and gam-
bits whenever they acquire a new partner. For those
of us in the know, it's tiresome, and so we drop hints,
don't you know."

Fidelity stopped, the flush deepening. She'd
known everyone was staring, but *this*... If only the ballroom floor would open beneath her. "I wish someone
had dropped those hints earlier."

Blue Tailcoat paused beside her, settling his free
hand atop her fingers where they rested on his forearm. "Would you have done anything differently?"

Silly question. And she'd thought him so generous, too. But when she opened her mouth to answer,
he rushed on.

"Because I've had such a lovely evening tonight."

Surprised, she froze and stared. He looked back,
somehow making her more aware of him than she'd
been before. It wasn't that he stood too close, for he
didn't, nor that he leered or fawned over her. But
some expression in his eyes, something hungry and
deep and so very, insanely happy, pulled her into his
gaze as if drawing her through a door.

A truly amazing door, one she couldn't believe
she'd never stepped through before.

He drew in a deep breath before continuing. Drawing in courage? "The most wonderful dance ever. The most beautiful, the most delightful partner." Gentle fingers pressed hers. The first strains of the next, something sweet and haunting, flowed around them like warm water. "Of course it's horrid if your evening hasn't been as splendid—"

She shook her head. "Not horrid — well, certain parts of it—"

He guffawed. "Doubtless."

"Do not laugh at me. There have been moments—"

His guffaw turned into a snicker. Something about the curl of his lips hitched her breath in her throat and set her pulse to pounding. Perhaps she should recognize him. But whoever he was, she didn't really know him, not properly.

The sweet, haunting music segued into the Sussex Waltz. Fidelity paused and glanced back. Couples were forming on the dance floor — *couples*, standing apart and private from any others, not the facing lines of country dancing. It could only be a waltz, a true turning waltz. She couldn't stifle her gasp. She'd secretly wished to try the turning waltz, even if it did border on scandalous. Now the opportunity presented and she had no partner.

Oh, if only she'd waited out *Miss Moore's Rant!* Then when Blue Tailcoat — delightful man — had come to claim her, they could have indulged her fancy together. As the situation stood, she'd already danced twice with Brightenburg; two with another man could be considered even more scandalous than the turning waltz.

She'd outsmarted herself, and it stung.

Perhaps her yearning showed — *perhaps nothing, I'm practically leaning toward the dance floor* — for Blue Tailcoat's smile again turned impish. "I wouldn't want to damage your reputation by leading you into temptation. But that sounds wonderful, and it could only be so with your company."

Generous man. Her heart warmed further. "It does, doesn't it?" The strains entwined around her, delectable, haunting, and they fed her yearning. She'd seen no sign that anyone recognized her, not even Clarissa — Jessica and Georgette didn't count — so what reason could there be for refusing? Blue Tailcoat had shown himself to be a true gentleman and an excellent dancer; who better for indulging a secret, scandalous fancy? "Yes. Yes, it does."

His smile deepened, from delighted to intimate, and his hand pressed hers once more. Fidelity shivered, his appreciation seeping into her core. Gently he turned her back to the ballroom floor.

Let the whispers begin. Delight rushed through her and Fidelity smiled. This time, she refused to care.

His smile quirked again, not apologetically but with exquisite intent. Other couples joined them, forming a loose line across the ballroom, white and black on one side, dusky pink and maroon on the other. Blue Tailcoat's gaze never left hers; that was demanded by the turning waltz, of course, and one of the reasons it was considered scandalous. But there seemed to be more in the steadiness of his gaze than anything taught by a dance master — more intimate, more personal. More...

The music changed and the dance began. They advanced a step, until only a breath separated their bodies, her skirt rustling against his silk stockings, then they retreated, advanced again and joined hands, turning a full circle around each other. His gaze never left hers. Yes, more; more intensity, more...

He settled his hand on her waist — *her waist!* — and drew hers to his. Sparks flared across her skin from his touch, not the intrusive shock Brightenburg had created but something comfortable and trust-worthy. Their free hands joined overhead and beneath that mutual grasp they continued turning, another full circle, a third. The colors to either side flowed together in the corners of her vision like a watercolor in the rain. Somehow their arms lowered and their hands clasped, right to right and left to left, and they advanced side by side, retreated, advanced again, and still he never looked away.

But more than her surroundings, more than the other dancers, Fidelity sensed the depth of Blue Tailcoat's esteem, evident in his every gesture from his smile to his gentle touch. It all added together — the haunting warmth in his never-shifting gaze, the close-ness of their bodies as they turned, the unabashed heat washing from him to her, the sweet pressure of their entangled arms — into an emotional abandon-ment like that of lovers.

It was intoxicating. But more mellow than the unhappy result of wine or spirits; more of a floating, exalted sensation, a relaxed dreaminess that settled around and through her and softened the edges of her vision. Staring into each other's eyes, arms entwined, bodies nearly touching, the barest pressure of his hand on her waist guided her motions and together they turned across the softness of a luscious dream-scape.

Then Blue Tailcoat glanced aside. He scowled.

For an odd, unbalanced moment, everything seemed wrong. She'd grown comfortable with his charm; his scowl carried a fearsome edge, like a mannerly horse suddenly flattening back its ears. It broke the dream's perfection. Fidelity shook her head, shook away the heaviness, and followed his gaze.

Deep puce, the shade of a dusky rose. Turning

slowly in place, held there by maroon bands — no, by maroon sleeves, a man wearing a maroon swallowtail. Only one woman in attendance wore a gown of that shade.

And only one man snugged his partner that scandalously close to his body.

Fidelity shivered.

Brightenburg and Jessica circled around each other, their hips glued together. Their clasped hands formed an arch above their heads, like a bower, and their hands at each other's waist couldn't clutch any tighter. The pink flush in the girl's cheeks glowed more brightly than her gown; her eyes sparkled, brilliant sapphires beneath the candlelight.

A movement on Jessica's waist, a flexing of fingers. Then Brightenburg's hand crawled up her side, paused, slid back down. The wrinkles smoothed from her muslin bodice, then vertical lines formed; he pressed against her so hard that his fingers stretched the beleaguered cloth. And he didn't stop at her waist. Jessica tucked her chin, coy lashes flickering and lips curling, and Brightenburg's nostrils flared.

Without thinking, Fidelity kept dancing, turning with Blue Tailcoat, her chin on her shoulder. But her heart pounded, horror rising in her throat. Something. She had to do something, break them apart, cause a scene, anything that would remove his hand from Jessica's hip. Anything that would protect her cousin from being seduced and ruined in public.

From making the same mistake Fidelity had considered making.

How had she ever been so foolish?

Fidelity's turning steps, under the gentle guidance of Blue Tailcoat's feather-light hand on her waist, finally rotated the budding scandal from her line of sight. She whipped her head around — she had to see, had to protect Jessica — but a hiss stopped her mid-whirl. For a moment she thought it had been a candle flame spurting, but Blue Tailcoat's steady gaze attracted and held hers without flinching. No, that hadn't been a flame — silly thought, with no candles near. That had been her partner seeking her attention. He'd noticed Brightenburg's disgraceful behavior, too, and judging from his narrowed eyes and pursed lips, he liked it not.

Fidelity leaned closer and whispered. "What should we do? I can't let him—"

His headshake stopped her. "We mustn't draw attention," he said, his voice a gentle murmur. "The dance will only last a few more minutes. When it ends—"

Of course, attracting attention to the situation would only make it worse. Clear-headed man, and discreet, as well. He could have reminded her that her dance with Brightenburg had been almost as eyebrow-raising. She'd emerged unscathed from the temptation, reputation, body, and soul, and when the music ended, she'd extricate Jessica, too.

Granted, everybody in the ballroom was watching and probably already gossiping. But if nipped off quickly, the situation could still be lived down; if a fuss were made...

Fidelity shuddered and nodded.

His smile deepened and warmed, easing her tension. Beneath his gaze, her every nerve ending tingled, fully aware of his attention, his regard, his physical nearness. Could he see into her soul? More importantly, did he want to?

When she shivered again, it had nothing to do with Brightenburg and everything to do with Blue Tailcoat.

Then the music rose to a string-filled crescendo.

A gentle touch on her waist sent her spinning; a firm clasp, holding her hand in an arch above their heads, kept her in place. The room dissolved into streaky motion and colors whirled past, ice white muslin, cherry wood paneling, candle flames and expensive green silk, then the touch stilled her, the clasp steadied her, and the music purred down to silence.

Leaving her staring into her partner's clear green eyes, intense, soulful, and... and yearning.

Loving?

Fidelity froze as the meaning behind his heartfelt gaze hammered home within her. This wasn't a man who wanted a scandalous fling, a dalliance behind the shrubbery or a tumble in a dark, private room. He wanted so much more than that. If the emotion he made no move to hide spoke truth, he wanted all of her, beginning with her heart.

And oh, how it hammered at the thought.

Then he blinked, glanced aside, and Fidelity realized she'd seen no dusky pink during that last, swirling turn. She stepped from Blue Tailcoat's arms, ignoring the applause from the other dancers, and glanced over her shoulder.

Jessica and Brightenburg were gone.

8

"Don't panic." Without moving his head, Blue Tail-coat glanced around the ballroom. His lips thinned. "I'll check the front and make certain no carriage has been called." His eyes returned to hers. All softness had faded away, and Fidelity breathed again; with such a man assisting her, Jessica might yet be rescued. "Check the back gardens."

Even as she nodded, he turned away, slid into the milling crush, and vanished.

Panic subdued but still simmering, Fidelity scanned the dancers and bystanders as she retraced her steps toward the seating area. No dusky rose along the forming dance line; not near the musicians, nor the refreshment tables, nor the card room doors. A flash of black in a herd of redcoats, and there stood the sober old black Melton. Her hope rose; Grey would be an excellent help in the crisis — but the hair above the black half-mask was shot with grey, shimmering in the chandeliers' light. She'd been wrong yet again and hadn't recognized her family's closest friend.

Some message hovered at the back of her mind, something she couldn't quite pinpoint.

But before she could suss it out, a swoop of yellow caught her eye. Georgette hesitated at the doorway to the rear gardens, her primrose gown swirling around her feet. Their gazes meshed across the ballroom and the crowd began to fall away, fading and hushing as if they no longer existed. Fidelity forced herself to continue her steady pace, one genteel step after the next, when all she wanted to do was break into a gallop and rush into battle. For something close to terror twisted Georgette's face. She glanced through the open doors, back to Fidelity, again through the doors...

Careful. Don't attract attention. Fidelity shook open her fan and fluttered it casually, hiding her surely fearful expression. The distance to the doors melted away. A lively reel began and the crowd surged toward the dance floor. With the crush falling away she let her pace quicken until she strode in tempo with the music. Had anyone else seen that silent scream for help? Would Grey follow, if he saw? Georgette glanced again through the back doors and this time didn't look away, one hand covering her mouth.

Fidelity slid her hand around the girl's shoulders and pulled her close. The back doors led to a patio, bricked terraces falling away toward the river. Lanterns hung from the trees, their red glow lighting free-standing brick walls dotted with shelves and potted plants, a knot garden surrounded by low bushes, higher bushes blocking the view, a preening peacock topiary with hothouse begonias coloring its tail. Too many places to look; the worst could happen before—

"Where are they?"

"Oh, Fi—" Georgette grabbed her arm and

dragged her through the door. "I saw— he—"

Down the first terrace, toward the first brick wall. A noise, a whimper, somewhere off in the dark? Fidelity's blood froze and fury drove out horror. If Jessica was hurt, she'd gladly lose every claim to a calm, serene, unflappable temperament, so long as Brightenburg paid for his crimes. Surely Grey had seen her run off; surely he'd follow and help her. Surely they'd be in time.

"Where?"

"This way." Her other hand hiking her skirt, Georgette danced down the brick layers and ran past the peacock. "They went— then he—"

Begonias spilled from clay pots, their sweet, spicy perfume flooding her lungs. Several pots stood on each brick wall, and Georgette and she swished past the plants, away from the lantern light and into the shadows. Another whimper. Fidelity pushed Georgette aside and peered around the last corner.

In the casual shelter of an evergreen bush, a luscious form pressed hips-first against the outer wall. Muslin splayed against the bricks beside his white-stockinged calves; he had her pinned and leaned against her. Fidelity's fury turned cold. She couldn't see the girl's face behind those broad shoulders, not even her hair, but there was no doubt of the victim's identity, nor that she fought against his enforced attentions. Without breaking the kiss, Brightenburg jerked Jessica's hands above their heads with one of his, and the other— the other—

Even her rage froze away. Fidelity dropped the fan, grabbed the closest clay pot, and smashed it down over Brightenburg's head.

Dirt and shards rained over his hair, his shoulders. He crumpled where he stood, a stem of flowers trailing across his back. Fidelity yanked Jessica away, thrust the girl behind her, and hefted another pot — just in case. "Mister Brightenburg, how dare you?"

Was he dead? No, more's the pity; he stirred on the brick pathway, shaking his head and fumbling to push himself to hands and knees. The flowers on his back fell away; so did his mask. Fidelity took aim, the fired clay heavy in her grip. Would she always remember this moment whenever she smelled begonias?

"Such behavior is an affront to all women everywhere." She didn't bother to keep her voice low or soft. Her invented, boring persona could go hang. "This young lady has done nothing to deserve your reprehensible attentions. She is my responsibility and my friend, and I will not allow you to harm her."

With a quick twist, Brightenburg rolled away and staggered up. A dark wetness trickled down the side of his face and dripped to his coat, colorless in the winter night's shadows. "Blast your eyes, you ruddy—"

Heart thudding, Fidelity stepped back, her clumsy weapon poised. But footsteps pounded up the brick path. A man ripped around the corner — *Blue Tailcoat, thank heavens* — took in the scene with a swift glance, and slid to a stop before Brightenburg, shielding Fidelity and the girls with his own body.

Brightenburg stumbled back a step. "—you ruddy b—"

Before he could complete the insult, Blue Tailcoat's fist flashed out. It buried itself into Brightenburg's nose with a surprisingly loud crunch. Brightenburg's head whipped back and he collapsed again, thudding onto the brick pathway, pretty much back where he'd started.

"Surely even your decadence wouldn't stretch to insulting a lady, Brightenburg."

That voice. *That voice.*

Again Brightenburg staggered up, shaking his

head like a confused bull. More dark liquid dripped from his nose, covering his swollen mouth. He glared at their protector. "What was that for?"

"Emily Cross," Blue Tailcoat said, his tone grim. His fist rose again. "And this one's for—"

But Brightenburg lurched aside out of reach, slamming his shoulder against the outer wall. He gripped the brick for balance and swayed forward. "Look, you—"

A thrown disk smacked into his cheek — a drainage saucer for a clay pot. He staggered again, and another saucer hit his chest. Jessica and Georgette stood at Fidelity's shoulders, each gripping more saucers, and a rush of pride swept through her. *Her* girls.

Blue Tailcoat's fist hadn't lowered. "I'm happy to offer you satisfaction. Will I be hearing from your second?"

With a snarl, Brightenburg wiped blood from his chin, turned, and stalked away into the night.

* * * *

Fidelity set the pot down — amazing that the poor begonia had survived her not-so-tender attentions — dusted off her hands, and pulled her girls into a tight embrace.

"I'm sorry." Jessica's face crumpled and her voice vanished into a wail. "I knew I shouldn't leave with him, but—"

"You can be no more sorry than I." A kiss to each smooth cheek, both remarkably dry, and Fidelity tightened the embrace. "You did nothing but follow my own despicable example, and if anything had happened to you, it would have been my fault. Can you forgive me?"

"Forgive *you?*" Jessica pulled back, her eyes enormous. "When I wanted so much to hurt you? You did nothing—"

"—except set the entire ridiculous train in motion." Another kiss, a warm glance with her heart in her eyes. "I think we've both wised up, but I am so very sorry for the fright you've suffered."

Georgette squeezed them both back together into a pile of warmth. "If you like, we can leave early."

Fidelity paused. She didn't want to. She wanted to stay and dance again with Blue Tailcoat, figure out who that remarkable man was — he'd withdrawn to the lantern light's edge, letting them sort themselves out in secure privacy, generous man. She wanted to suffuse herself in his appreciation and learn more of his gentlemanlike ways. But perhaps it would be for the best. Surely she'd find him again. And surely Jessica needed quiet and peace to fully recover.

But a light flared in those blue eyes and Jessica's chin lifted. Still no tears dampened her face. "I've never left a ball early in my life and I won't start now in compliment to *him.*"

The giggles couldn't be stopped. "You silly girl. You're brave and beautiful and I'm so proud to be your cousin."

"Really?" Georgette nudged Jessica, eyes wide behind her half-mask. "If you're certain—"

"Of course I am," Jessica said.

"—then now's the time to take advantage of the situation."

They giggled together. "You're right." And Jessica smiled.

More hugs, then Fidelity helped the girls repin their curls. Repositioning her sardonyx brooch hid the torn lace at Jessica's neckline, and they checked each other's masks, ensuring they were firmly in place.

Then, arm in arm, with sweet words of gratitude in passing, the girls slipped past Blue Tailcoat, into the spilled lantern light, and vanished down the path toward the house.

He turned. A flame's red glow flickered across his black half-mask, glinted from his eye. His smile had finally worn away, only the edges of his lips turning up. Fidelity's breathing stopped, her heart a second later. They were alone, in the back garden's farthest corner, just as she'd planned for the evening to end.

Had they done that deliberately? Those little minxes.

She should follow them. Right now, without delay. Really, it would be for the best. But her feet disliked the idea. They refused to budge and before she could convince them, he touched her arm with his fingertips and every thought dissipated from her head.

Her heart resumed, with a strange, too-slow thudding. Still she couldn't move, and so his hand trailed up her arm, the gentlest of pressure along her glove's outer edge. For a moment he touched bare skin, between glove and sleeve, and she quivered. The touch removed itself immediately and she wished it back — *oh, she wanted it back* — but it didn't return. Instead, she felt the very air move as his fingers continued their path, a half-inch from her arm, up to her shoulder, up—

And suddenly she knew his intention. Her heart leaped, but still she couldn't move. So she stood like a statue, like a useless lump of shivering marble, as his fingers curled around the edge of her mask and lifted it up, not off her face but past her mouth—

He eased close, closer, until all she could see was him, his green eyes intense behind his half-mask, cheeks darkened with a beard's early shadow, straight nose, soft lips. The slow thumping of her heart accelerated. Cold drove out her lingering warmth then in turn it surrendered to more warmth as he came even closer, then he leaned forward and she closed her eyes.

Soft and gentle, the touch of his lips to hers. The cold vanished again and a heated flush spread from his kiss, from some hidden place deep inside her. The two heat sources met in her chest and exploded like a supernova. Stars fell around her, behind her closed eyelids, stars shooting and burning, blinding galaxies and zinging comets, and he wasn't even kissing her hard. He was holding back, letting her set the pace.

Fidelity leaned in and grasped his arms, turning her head and deepening the kiss instinctively.

There, the pressure she'd wanted, the delicious warmth spreading to her restless hands. Solidity behind her, the spicy sweetness of begonias falling around them; he'd backed her into the freestanding brick wall, pressed her there gently, and the softness brushing her ear wasn't her hair but a thick, furry leaf. She opened her mouth, ready for more—

—and someone giggled. No, two someones.

Little *minxes*.

Aggrieved, Fidelity disengaged and glanced back along the path. Two squirming shadows leaned together beside the preening peacock topiary. Well, perhaps the situation had progressed far enough. For the moment, at least.

But there was one question which had to be answered immediately. She swept off his mask. He didn't try to stop her.

And she realized she should have known all along. In all honesty, part of her had known; hadn't she thought of him, not as Blue Tailcoat but by his proper name, as she and Georgette had raced through the garden's secrets to Jessica's rescue? Hadn't she yearned then for him to see her need for him, to follow and rescue her, as well as the girls? Hadn't he always been the answer she'd sought, the one she hadn't recognized even when he stood before her?

Grey cleared his throat. "I've been waiting for you to notice me." The mask slid from her face the rest of the way, and he leaned his forehead against hers. "Instead of him."

Fidelity caressed his cheek, the hint of stubble scraping beneath her gloved fingertips. "I should have worn this dress sooner."

His eyebrows crinkled. "Well, it's — it's a beautiful dress, one of the loveliest I've ever seen, but I don't quite see—"

She shook her head. "It was meant to hide my identity. Instead, it set me free."

"From Brightenburg's influence?"

"From my own."

The little minxes could go hang. Fidelity leaned in for another kiss.

Epilogue

four more days later,
Sunday, December 19, 1813

Fidelity stretched out her sewing, repositioning the ivory gown's unhemmed skirt and tucking the finished bits underneath, out of the way. The morning room's little fire crackled brightly, an able ally against the cold drizzle falling outside, and with its warmth driving away the chill the last of her happiness fell into place. Was being so contented some sort of crime? It certainly felt unusual.

On her right, Georgette stitched an ivory sleeve with cautious precision. On her left, Jessica's attempted imitation of her sister's sewing — well, at least the girl was trying. Two weeks ago, if handed a needle and thread, she'd have whined and pouted instead.

Perhaps Jessica felt Fidelity's amused stare, for she dropped her hands into her lap and heaved a monstrous sigh. "Fi, I can perfectly understand wanting a new gown for your wedding. It's the height of good taste, starting your new life in a new gown, and every young woman should follow your example. But making it yourself?"

Fidelity let her smile break free. Someday, that girl was going to... make some lucky man very poor indeed, and enrich every seamstress in town and country both. "Well, I can hardly wear the blue one into church, now, can I?"

A suppressed giggle from Georgette's chair. "May I?"

Jessica snorted. And that quickly, all three of them were giggling away like schoolgirls sneaking into the larder to steal butter biscuits. It felt so good, letting herself go and laughing with her cousins, that Fidelity rocked back in her chair and let the sewing wait while she en-joyed the moment.

A soft voice spoke from the corner by the window. "Mayhap my bride-to-be will wear that gorgeous gown to the Christmas Eve ball."

Fidelity glanced up. Over the top of an opened newspaper peered a pair of clear green eyes, twinkling with mischief. She held his stare, even though it skewered her from across the room and melted her with his warmth.

No, that wasn't a newspaper. It was a broadsheet. Grey read the gossip, doubtless learning what everyone had to say about the Maynards' masked ball.

She swallowed. "But if I wear the blue gown, then everyone will know—"

"—that I roundly defeated Sylvestre Brightenburg in the only competition that matters — the one for your hand." The twinkle in his eyes gave way to a possessive glow. "And that I'm getting ready to claim my prize."

Heat touched her cheeks. But she couldn't look

away, and Fidelity rolled her lips together. "Is there anything in the papers about him?"

She knew she didn't have to be any more specific. Beside her, Jessica froze over her next stitch. She'd reacted that way ever since the masked ball, whenever *that name* was mentioned. But at the Maynards' she'd stayed and danced all night long, finishing the evening on the arm of Tate the younger, son of the Earl of Danvers, and everyone in the know had agreed it was a fitting conclusion.

Grey folded the broadsheet. "There's a vague report of a dreadful accident, but no details, of course. It seems certain he's left for the country to recover."

Jessica's shoulders slumped, and Fidelity shared her relief with a small sigh. "Then yes, my husband-to-be, I'll wear the blue gown on Christmas Eve for your triumphal march." *And make some scandalous memories with you to last us the rest of our lives together.*

A scowl lowered Grey's brows. "My love, I hope I've proven you've no reason to fear that—"

Heavens only knew what word he'd intended to say. Hurriedly she cut him off before he reached it. "Of course you have. But he's a predator and you can't protect every young woman there." She squeezed Jessica's forearm, and received a grateful sidelong glance in return.

Grey's scowl faded away. "Good point."

"Indeed, yes." Georgette's sewing sat ignored in her lap, her thumb stroking the ivory silk, back and forth, back and forth, as if mesmerized. "Mis-ter Bright-en-burg—" and her singsong voice no longer held any admiration, only scorn "—remains a problem."

"No longer our problem, though." Blue eyes squinting, Jessica stabbed her needle home in a stitch that doubtless would need to be reworked. "He's gone, and good riddance."

But as a solution, a simple relocation wasn't sufficient; there were young ladies in the country, too, and the man — *not gentleman* — in question could attack someone there as easily as in Mayfair. They needed a permanent answer to the Brightenburg danger, and in a rush, Fidelity knew what that answer had to be. "Someday I hope he finds someone to love, too."

The scoffing sound from Georgette earned another giggle-snort from Jessica. "You're too generous by far," Georgette said.

"No, when he finds real love, a wife, someone to stand beside him — then the young women of Mayfair should be safer. It's possible that nothing will ever tame him entirely, but it's also possible that true love will." *True love...* Fidelity couldn't restrain her glance across the room. He watched her — *well, of course he did* — and the gleam in his eyes matched the melting sensation in her heart. She'd been blind and foolish for so long, but despite herself she'd been found by her own true love, and she reveled in the finding.

And if she kept staring at him, she'd create all new methods of embarrassing herself. Fidelity nodded at the sleeve Jessica held. "Are you going to finish that or just stare at it?"

Another sideways glance, this one devoid of anything approaching gratitude. "I'm going to stare at it—"

"—and I'm going to stare at *you*." Grey rose, set the folded broadsheet aside, and crossed the room toward them.

Around her, the room faded away, leaving Fidelity alone in a muffled and foggy cocoon. Only Grey, her very own Grey, shared the space with her, and as he approached, the cocoon shrank, enfolding them together in its silence and nearness. He took her hand and drew her to her feet, took the unfinished ivory gown and set it aside, then tucked her close against him, closer, even closer, and as their lips met she let her eyes drift shut.

When she finally surfaced to breathe, air having become scarce and unfortunately necessary, the morning room truly was empty. The girls had vanished and closed the door behind him.

"Those little minxes," she said. "They're supposed to be our chaperones." But she couldn't really be angry, not when presented with the opportunity to rest her head upon Grey's chest and listen to his heart beating, hard and fast.

Her Grey. Her very own.

"Well." His voice rumbled through her, a sensuous vibration, and she shivered in response. "They *were* our chaperones... until they and I made a deal, that is."

She pressed her lips together to stop the laughter. "This deal better not have anything to do with my blue gown."

"Mmmm-noooo. Not directly, at least." His arms tightened around her, one hand stroking her hair in the most delightful and distracting manner. "But they really want to learn where you bought the material, who sewed it, how much it would cost for two more to be made..."

A distracting manner, indeed. Had he counted on that effect? "And you believe you can convince me to share that information?"

The hand stroked down her hair, down her neck, her back, and her shivering intensified. Again he leaned closer and her eyes drifted closed. "I can try, can't I?"

About the Author

Vivian Roycroft is a pseudonym for historical fiction and adventure writer J. Gunnar Grey. And if she's not careful, her pseudonymous pseudonym will have its own pseudonym soon, too. Plus an e-reader, a yarn stash, an old Hermès hunt saddle, and a turtle sundae at Culver's.

You can find Vivian and her writing compadre, J.L. Salter, at their shared blog, taketwoonromance.weebly.com/, or follow her on Twitter as @VivianRoycroft.

Looking for more quality Regencies?

Shirley Raye Redmond

Prudence Pursued

At the advanced age of twenty-seven, vicar's daughter Prudence Pentrye is on the shelf. Content to occupy her time by attending meetings of Mr. Wilberforce's Abolition Society and helping her father administer vaccines in an effort to prevent a small pox epidemic, Prudence is resolved to see that her younger cousin Margaret does not share her own unmarried fate.

But Margaret is plain and shy. She is repulsed when a swashbuckling baronet, Sir James Brownell, makes her an offer of marriage. With his sunburned skin, eye patch, and indifference to fashion, Sir James is not Margaret's idea of a romantic suitor. Nor does Margaret enjoy his tales of fighting against Malay pirates and trekking through tropical jungles on the island of Borneo in hopes of capturing a living orangutan.

Prudence, however, finds herself secretly smitten. Will she maintain control of her traitorous heart or will she trust God to make her life richer and more rewarding than the one she had planned for herself?

A sweet and sometimes inspirational Regency romance

Heather Gray

Jackal

Hiding in the shadows just got harder.

When tragedy strikes, Juliana and her family must flee their home. Can they persuade a virtual stranger to help them? Juliana isn't so sure, especially after their chaperone threatens to cane him. Even as Juliana struggles to trust him, she finds herself drawn to this mysterious man. Surely all she wants from him is refuge...

Rupert is a man whose life depends on his ability to remain unnoticed. What, then, is he supposed to do with this family he's inherited? His life is overrun with an ancient chaperone who would terrify a lesser man, two spirited girls, and the secretive Juliana — someone he comes to think of as his own precious jewel.

With this new responsibility thrust upon him, Rupert will have to make sacrifices — but will God ask him to sacrifice everything?

An inspirational young adult Regency romantic suspense by a bestselling author

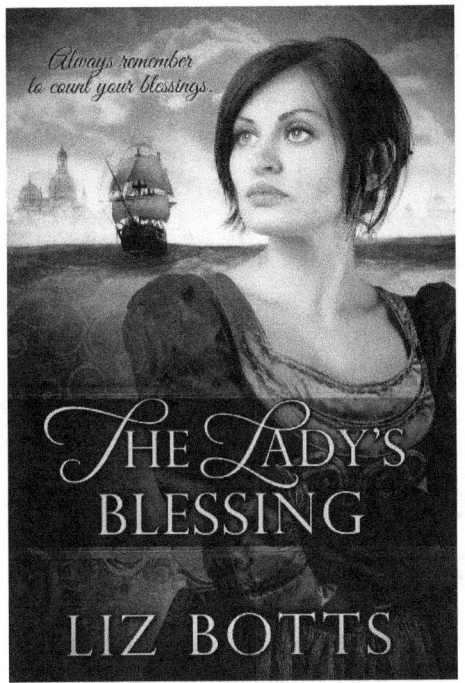

Liz Botts

The Lady's Blessing

In May of 1812, American militiamen raid Felicity Hawthorne's home in British Canada. Life as she knows it ends: her mother is killed, her brother is taken captive, and her father is injured. In a matter of weeks her father decides to send her to England to live with her mother's parents. He sends her in the care of Lord Graham Blessington, who has been serving in the Royal Navy as he runs away from the pain of his life back home.

After an eventful sea voyage, fate intervenes,

allowing Graham and Felicity the chance to spend more time together, along with his small daughter. As she becomes deeply attached to the pair, Felicity must decide if she will go back to London to submit to social expectations or if she will follow her heart.

A sweet young adult Regency romantic suspense

Kay Springsteen

Teach Me Under the Mistletoe

According to Caroline "Kitty" Tyndall's friends, a young lady who's gone two seasons in London with nary a nibble from a prospective suitor is well on the way to spinsterhood. But what's a girl to do when she's never been kissed, and the worldly man she wants regards her as a child?

Hugh McCollum spends his days as a stable hand staying out of trouble and saving for his planned emigration to America. When Lady Caroline asks him to teach her how to kiss so the man she's set her cap for will find her more sophisticated, he knows he should run in the other direction. But when a pretty young woman falls into his arms and begs for his help, what's a red-blooded man to do but oblige?

If learning to kiss leads Kitty to love, will the man of her dreams be the man of her heart?

A sweet Regency by an international bestselling author

Christi Caldwell

A Marquess for Christmas

Lady Patrina Tidemore gave up on the ridiculous notion of true love after having her heart shattered and her trust destroyed by a black-hearted cad. Used as a pawn in a game of revenge against her brother, Patrina returns to London from a failed elopement with a tattered reputation and little hope for a respectable match. The only peace she finds is in her solitude on the cold winter days at Hyde Park. And even that is yanked from her by two little hellions who just happen to have a devastatingly handsome, but coldly aloof father, the Marquess of Beaufort. Something about the lord stirs the dreams she'd once carried for an honorable gentleman's love.

Weston Aldridge, the 4th Marquess of Beaufort, was deceived and betrayed by his late wife. In her faithlessness, he's come to view women as self-serving, indulgent creatures. Except, after a series of chance encounters with Patrina, he comes to appreciate how uniquely different she is than all women he's ever known.

At the Christmastide season, a time of hope and new beginnings, Patrina and Weston unexpectedly learn true love in one another. However, as Patrina's scandalous past threatens their future and the happiness of his children, they are both left to determine if love is enough.

A clean Regency by a bestselling author

Felicia Rogers

The Ruse

Luke Andrews, Baron of Stockport, is in trouble. He needs a wealthy bride to secure future funds for his financially shaky estate, but the belle of the London season is a spoiled terror with an arrogant father. They'd try the nerves of a saint and Luke can't quite bring himself to make an offer he knows he'd regret.

Meanwhile, Luke's half-brother Chadwick never could resist a good game of Faro, or anything else, for that matter. With the baron away, Chadwick will play

— gambling the estate's remaining funds into oblivion. He needs to devise his own scheme to replace the money he's lost, before his brother returns.

In Stockport village, Brigitta Blackburn doesn't have two sticks to rub together — literally. With the estate in financial distress and rents high, food and wood are scarce. When she sneaks onto the baron's land to steal some firewood, she's caught, hauled before the play-acting "baron," Chadwick, and offered a solution to her plight... and his.

But Chadwick's ruse embroils them all. How can Brigitta accept what she thinks to be true, when she really yearns to follow her heart?

A sweet and traditional Regency

Elizabeth Hanbury

Christmas at Rakehell Manor

A house of sin... shrouded in mystery and steeped in ever more scandalous gossip, where debauchery and wild parties are rumoured to take place.

A notorious rake... whose wicked reputation sends neighbours swooning over their tea cups. Can he really be as bad as he seems?

A lonely paid companion... whose prim and practical exterior hides a lush sensuality waiting to be awakened.

Prudence Eylesbarrow is resigned to dreary spinsterhood and to never finding love. All she wants is one Christmas where she's not at someone's beck and call.

But when Prue finds herself snowbound at the infamous Rakehell Manor, her curiosity with Hugo, Marquess of Warwick — mysterious, handsome, world-weary, cynical — tempts her to reveal passions she never knew she possessed. Even so Prue is under no illusions. It was a fool's game to think a penniless nobody could tame the master of Rakehell, for that way lay heartache and social ruin.

Or has the time come for the power of passion, the promise of love, and the magic of Christmas to unite two people from very different worlds?

A clean Regency by a bestselling author

Ruth J. Hartman

A Courtship for Cecilia

Cecilia Fletcher yearns for true love with the man of her heart. A life of her own away from her demanding mother would be an added benefit. But in order to do that, Cecilia must live a lie, making it necessary to use a false name in order to hide a family secret.

Barrington Radcliff was betrayed by a woman who he thought loved him. Because of that, trust is hard to willingly give. When he meets pretty Cecilia Fleming, his heart wants to give her a chance. Something about her doesn't ring true, but Barrington allows love to overrule his good judgment.

Can Cecilia and Barrington get past their hurt and secrets long enough to find true love?

A sweet Regency by a bestselling author

Nicole Zoltack

Love Before Honor

Honor. Truth. Loyalty. Love. All of these matter most to Sir Gerald. To avenge his love's death, he challenges her murderer to a duel. Her twin, however, feels that Alice never loved Gerald and gives him a tea. Alice had also given him teas, which enhanced his love for her, but this tea is different. This tea sends him into the future, to the Regency era.

Lady Vanessa seeks a Christmas treat when she hears something outside the manor. Upon investigation, she sees a man dressed in armor. Unwilling to turn away a confused man with the approaching holiday, she convinces her parents to house Gerald until the new year.

Scandal has forced Vanessa's parents to accept William, a rich suitor, as their daughter's best chance at marriage. But he does not understand her or her love of books and only sees her for her looks, whereas Gerald listens to her, confides in her and she in him. With the approaching holiday, nothing is certain — not whether Gerald can discover a way back to his duel, whether he can move on from Alice, and not whether this Christmas will be a happy one for either Gerald or Vanessa.

A sweet time-travel Regency romance

Kim Bowman

The Duke of Christmas Past

The only thing Donovan Ellis, Seventh Duke of Gatewood, wants for Christmas is for it to be over. Too much sadness surrounds the holiday. Horrors he'd prefer to forget. Oh, there's one present he yearns for with all his heart, but his foolishness pushed her into the arms of another. So if he can't have the one thing he truly desires, then he just wants to be left alone to drown in his own misery.

But when a ghostly apparition visits him, claiming things can be set right, can Donovan believe? Can he trust the Duke of Christmas Past? Or will meddling in the past bring more heartache than he already has to bear?

A sweet time-travel Regency romance

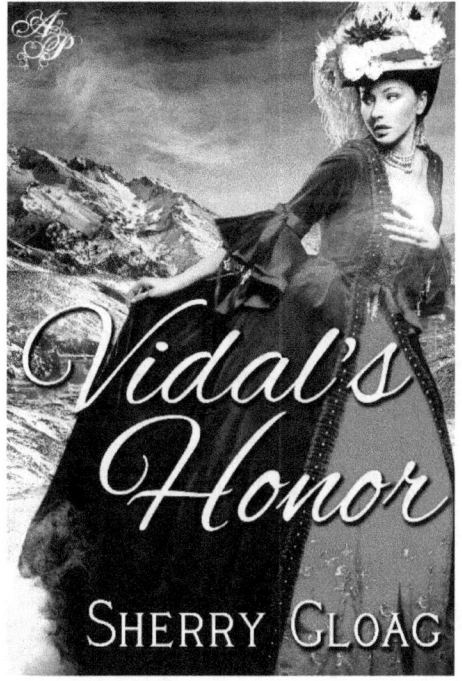

Sherry Gloag

Vidal's Honor

When plunged into a world of spies, agents and espionage during the Peninsula wars, Honor, Lady Beaumont, flees for her life when the French capture her husband at Salamanca, and relies on his batman to arrange her safe passage back to England.

Viscount Charles Vidal is ordered by Robert Dumas, the First Lord of the Admiralty, to travel to Spain and escort the only woman he's ever loved, Lord Devlin Beaumont's widow, back home before the French discover her whereabouts.

Their journey is fraught with danger, least of all knowing whether they are surrounded by friends or foe. Will they survive long enough to explore the possibility of a future together or will whispers of treason be enough to see Honor dispatched to Tyburn first?

A sweet Regency romantic suspense

Tempting the Earl

WENDY MAY ANDREWS

Wendy May Andrews

Tempting the Earl

Emily must masquerade as an earl's servant for reasons she's not willing to divulge. To her astonishment she finds she enjoys the role, but unfortunately finds herself attracted to the haughty young earl. He too struggles with an attraction to his beautiful new maid, but has his mind set on pursuing a courtship with the much more appropriate Lady Claire.

Who is Emily? Why is she hiding in the earl's household? Can a case of mistaken identity lead to true love?

A sweet Regency full-length novel

Also by Vivian Roycroft

writing as J. Gunnar Grey

The gorgeous woman leaned closer, almost into his personal space, her dark hair falling in gentle waves to her shoulders. Kennie glanced around, uncomfortable even in his fascination. But none of the joggers passing them seemed to notice her, and she wasn't a woman to be ignored.

"Do you believe in holiness?" she asked.

NATO Rapid Response sapper Captain Kenneth Rutland needs something to believe in. His life has gone too far off course, and he's easily sucked in when a beautiful stranger gives him a chance to escape his cynical, disappointing reality. She offers her hand and he takes it, not caring what awaits him.

But danger haunts Niviane's world and Kennie can't remain happily oblivious for long. Strange things happen, things his engineering logic can't explain. Evil lurks in the park and it's guarding an abomination. Somehow, even though they've only just met, Kennie's an important part of her mission to destroy that evil. Can he fight through the savagery and disbelief, and let the Christmas star work its healing miracle?

A paranormal inspirational Christmas novella

Thanks for reading! Dingbat Publishing strives to bring you quality entertainment that doesn't take itself too seriously. I mean honestly, with a name like that, our books have to be good or we're going to be laughed at. Or maybe both.

If you enjoyed this book, the best thing you can do is buy a million more copies and give them to all your friends... erm, leave a review on the readers' website of your preference. All authors love feedback and we take reviews from readers like you seriously.

Oh, and c'mon over to our website:
www.DingbatPublishing.Weebly.com

Who knows what other books you'll find there?

Cheers,
Gunnar Grey,
publisher, author, and Chief Dingbat

δ
Dingbat Publishing

www.ingramcontent.com/pod-product-compliance
Lightning Source LLC
Chambersburg PA
CBHW070635130626
46555CB00006B/2560